Dearest Mother
and Dad

Christina Thompson

ISBN: 9798630544896

Dearest Mother and Dad

Edited by C.K. Brooke
Cover Art by Ampersand Book Cover Designs
Cover Photograph: Christina's father with his parents
Visit ChristinaKThompson.com

ACKNOWLEDGEMENTS

To Mom, thank you for deciphering Dad's chicken scratch handwriting, in pencil, on see-through stationery. We learned his story together.

To my children, David and Andrea, thank you for the vacation to Zane's Landing in Manistee, Michigan where—after months of research—I finally outlined and started the first draft without distraction. The cabin in the woods surrounded by nature inspired me.

To the Otsego VFW Post #3030, thank you for your valuable insights and personal accounts.

To my wonderful editor, C.K. Brooke, thank you for your technical skills. Your encouragement on this project meant more than you'll ever know.

And, most of all, to my husband, Kraig, thank you for your unwavering support as my sounding board. You gave me the courage and strength to follow my heart.

In loving memory of Dad

To Patricia, James, and Jefrey,
May we have a deeper understanding of Dad

PROLOGUE

STANDING ALONE IN THE MIDDLE of his parents' living room, Matt Connor rubbed the back of his crew cut. *Where do I start?* Framed family pictures consumed every space on the walls. He couldn't tell what color the wallpaper was. Knickknacks gathered dust and cluttered the end tables, china cabinet, curios cabinets, shelves, and the hutch. *What am I supposed to do with all of this bric-a-brac?* He had so many questions, and he'd just buried the man who always had the answers.

His wife, Eva, and their seventeen-year-old son, David, were going to help him clean and prep the house to sell. The money would go into David's college fund. Matt didn't know what he'd do without Eva and David; they gave him solace after his parents' deaths.

David burst through the front door, balancing a stack of flattened packing boxes, a roll of tape, and Sunday's thick Kalamazoo Gazette. "Where do you want to start?" he asked his father, dumping his armload onto the living room carpet.

"Well," Matt replied, "we can donate the books to the library and then the collectables and clothes to the Salvation Army."

"That's a good start." Eva joined them from the kitchen. "I'll call the women's shelter to see what they need."

For the next week, the Connor family packed and delivered items to various nonprofit charity sites around town. By the end of the week, when the house had been virtually emptied, Matt and David carried up from the basement two worn-out cardboard boxes labeled "Orrin's stuff" in Matt's father's tidy cursive. They set the boxes in the middle of the empty living room floor. Eva had just returned, carrying in a large pizza and a six-pack of Coke.

David relieved her of the Cokes. "Last two boxes," he informed her.

Sitting on the floor, they ate their dinner. In between bites, David rummaged inside the first box. He pulled out a thick stack of faded envelopes held together by a pale pink ribbon.

"These are dated 1952," David said.

"Really?" Matt leaned over the other box. He picked up a picture of a General pinning a medal on what appeared to be his then-eighteen-year-old father, Orrin Connor, during the Korean War.

"Grandpa got a medal?" David asked. "For what?"

Eva opened the top letter as Matt stared at the photo. "I don't know," he replied. "Dad never talked about his experiences in Korea."

"He was a corpsman," Eva said, glancing at the letter.

"What's a corpsman?" David asked.

"Like a medic," she replied. "These are letters he mailed to his parents."

"Wow," David said. "Let's read some. I don't know much about that war."

Eva looked at Matt. "Are you up for this?"

Matt nodded and leaned back against the bare wall. "I'd like to know more, too."

CHAPTER ONE

23 November 1952

Dearest Mother and Dad,

I know you're disappointed in me for drinking. However, I am not becoming a drunkard and I did not chase after the dance hall girls. In my defense, I just finished eighteen weeks of basic field medical training at Portsmouth, VA and then specialized combat medical training at Fort Sam Houston in San Antonio. That's a lot of studying and it was only a couple of beers.

Mother, you shouldn't worry. I'm with a great bunch of guys. We always go out as a group, but I will watch out for shady characters wanting to take my money. You should know the Navy doesn't let us carry a lot of money so even if someone stole my wallet they wouldn't get much.

Today is our last day of our fifteen-day infantry training with the Marines at Camp Pendleton near San Diego. Sergeant Dixon Mayo, a real nice fellow, said we'll have an easy peasy day. Then, as a Navy Corpsman, I'll be part of the Fleet Marine Force.

Enclosed is a picture of me and my buddy Rawley Armstrong. Doesn't he look like that actor John Wayne from Rio Grande? Rawley acts tough and has a cocky swagger like John Wayne, but he's a good egg. He did his last run through the obstacle course yesterday. He actually finished before some of the Marines. Anyway, I'll write more tonight. I don't want to be late for my turn on the course.

All the love a son can give,

Orrin

Rawley

FROM THE DOORWAY OF THE barracks overlooking the obstacle course, I crossed my arms and shook my head. *Easy peasy*, Orrin had said. *Rawley, it can't be that bad*, he'd told me.

Well, after my turn yesterday, I tried to warn him. Now, the pounding rain blinded eighteen-year-old Orrin Connor as he crawled through the mud. His herringbone twill uniform, also called dungarees, went from olive drab to wet dirty brown. Two feet above the ground, a canopy of razor wire covered the quarter mile area.

For once, Orrin should be glad for his thin frame. He wiped his face, leaving a stream of dirt dripping down his chin. The firing of Marines' M1 carbines and Chinese burp guns over his head thundered with the downpour. I, for one, would forever remember those sounds.

Orrin's weapon dipped in and out of the mud while his medical pouch and three bandoliers periodically caught on the barbed wire. With a dozen Marines around him, he crept across the flooding obstacle course. The squad out-crawled him. Lagging behind, he winced when Sergeant Mayo stomped along the outside edge parallel to him.

I cringed as Mayo took a deep breath. "Connor, move your ass! By God, you're going to do this and you're going to like it!"

Short and stocky, the solid mass of a sergeant had a chip on his shoulder. His voice boomed louder than the gunfire. Even with all that yelling, he hadn't once started the day hoarse.

When a piece of razor wire snagged Orrin's bag again, he dropped his gun in the muddy water. With a groan, he yanked the medic bag, tearing the strap.

Someone howled, "Corpsman!"

From the barracks, I held my breath and watched Orrin raise his head then push the front of his crooked helmet above his brow. Standing at the end of the course, the Marines pointed to a downed man twenty feet in front of him. Leaving his gun, Orrin kept his medic bag above the mud and moved double-time. Cradling the bag, he knelt beside Alexander Marshall, clutching his shoulder. Orrin and I were slightly annoyed by the chiseled private who was a notorious ladies' man. The women didn't seem to mind. They still fawned over him and ignored the rest of us.

The thunder of gunfire abruptly stopped. The heavy showers, however, did not. The saturated Marines waited at the edge to the razor wire course. Using his body, Orrin shielded the wound from the rain. Leaning on the doorway of the barracks glad to be dry, I watched the drama unfold. Metal barbs bit into the back of Orrin's neck as he worked to access Marshall's shoulder. I've been bitten by those barbs once or twice so I knew it hurt.

"Corpsman! Get him out of there!" Mayo yelled, beet red and pacing into a bigger huff.

Orrin ignored him. Our training had taught us what to do and what not to do for each kind of wound.

Instead of acknowledging the sergeant, Orrin spoke calmly to the wounded man. "I can't move you yet. First, I need to see what the issue is."

"Connor! Pull him out! Now!" Mayo roared.

Marshall moved his hand. No wound existed. "Mayo's test to see how you respond."

With a nod, Orrin crossed the Marine's arms on his chest, laying Marshall's gun at an angle atop him, too. Unable to stand up due to the razor wire, he tugged the collar, moving him an inch in the rising water of the lowland course. The sharp barbs snagged his clothes and his straps, yanking him backward multiple times. He had to fix his crooked helmet often. After twenty minutes, he had only pulled him two feet. I thought Orrin could float him the twenty yards in the pond of mud. Apparently not.

Finally, Sergeant Mayo threw up his hands. "Marshall, out!"

The Marine flipped onto his abdomen, splashing the water, and quickly crawled out. Drenched, Orrin sighed and followed. The sergeant looked as though he was gearing up for a dressing down. We both disliked being yelled at, but then who did?

Exiting the course on his knees, Orrin started to stand, but the razor wire caught his pant leg. I cringed as he lost his balance and fell face first into the mud puddle. That had to be a mouth full of grit.

As soon as he stood up, Sergeant Mayo lit into him. The others waited as if Orrin's reprimand might make up for their soaked bodies in the downpour that had yet to lessen. I had heard that California's weather would be all sunshine. What a disappointment! Michigan's weather was better. At least it had four seasons.

"You're a Grade-A klutz! How the hell do you expect to save my Marines' lives, you scrawny squid?" Mayo demanded.

"Adapting," Orrin replied at attention.

I smiled at his answer. Ignoring the rain, Sergeant Mayo did not smile. He stared at him, dumbfounded by the answer, an answer that he had lectured about from the start of our two-week crash course.

Mayo clenched his jaw. "I hope to God you figure it out before your first patrol."

"I won't let them down."

Mayo walked away, leaving a dozen men standing in the rain, probably wondering if they could finally dry off. As the Marines rushed in my direction, I retreated to the back corner of the rows of bunks, two beds high, and jumped onto the top one. I picked up where I left off in my letter beside a snapshot of my twin. At twenty, my sister had blue eyes like me. I'd have wavy brown hair like hers too, if it wasn't for my buzz cut.

I spoke my mind here, which got me into trouble. My arms were pretty strong now with all the pushups they made me do. I wouldn't tolerate stupidity, especially if I was drunk and in a bar with men bigger, dumber, and more muscular than I was. Although he was naïve, Orrin had my back and could be scrappy in a fight like a cornered wolverine. I was a bad influence on him. I thought he liked it, though. Just because we came from different backgrounds didn't mean we can't be friends.

After a lukewarm shower in the barracks of the 1st Marine Division of George Company, Orrin held a washcloth against the back of his neck. "Would you slap a Band-Aid on my neck? I can't reach it." He turned his back and pulled the bloody washcloth away from the area.

"I saw you stand at attention in the middle of the course."

"Yes. That's exactly what I did."

"Well, you'll need a stitch or two. Good thing you know a guy."

"Do it before the sergeant comes in," Orrin replied.

I slid off my bunk, grabbed my medical bag, then pointed to the edge of the lower rack. Orrin moved his muddy clothes, stationery, and his corpsman bag aside and sat. He was a constant slob. The Navy couldn't drill it out of him and apparently the Marines couldn't, either. With all the pushup punishments, he should have huge biceps by now, but he didn't.

"I wonder if you can put in for a Purple Heart." With a smirk, I cleaned the back of his neck with alcohol.

"It's a papercut." He winced at the sting. "I hate being called a *squid*."

"It'll fade someday." I laughed then sobered. "Aren't you nervous? We only had two weeks of infantry training."

"We'll be too busy doing grunt-work at Battalion Reserve to even load our guns, right?" Orrin replied.

His casual attitude calmed my anxiety. Orrin still needed to figure out how to adapt in the field, though. We knew we'd be on the frontline at some point.

In the chow line, Orrin and I picked up metal trays and silverware. Corporals Brian McClellan and Dale Kaminski cut in front of us. Sergeant Mayo mixed up their names all the time because they looked like twins—same physical build, same nondescript looks.

"Gentlemen, the line's back there," I said in a sweet voice dripping with sarcasm.

"I don't know what you mean, squid," McClellan replied.

"We outrank you," Kaminski added.

"No, you don't. We're E-4s, too," I replied with my dander up. The corporals laughed and continued down the line.

Under Sergeant Mayo's glare, Orrin put his hand on my shoulder. "I'm over it. They'll respect us soon enough," Orrin mumbled.

While two privates behind the counter slapped mashed potatoes, gravy, meatloaf, and green beans onto our trays, Orrin and I observed McClellan trying to hide his limp. A possible foot issue? Studying anatomy and physiology, we practiced watching the gaits and movements of Marine and Navy personnel. Did they have back pain, knee pain, foot pain? A diagnosis of sorts.

"McClellan's limping," Orrin said under his breath.

"My pleasure to stomp on his foot. Accidently, of course."

Orrin snorted. "This is our job. Let's not make enemies just yet."

"Fine. I'll distract Kaminski so you can talk to him. A dollar says he won't tell you anything."

"Deal."

In the loud, crowded room, I set my tray between them and elbowed my way into the tight spot. Glaring at me, the corporals slid apart. Their movement made room for Orrin, who sat next to McClellan and me.

Orrin lowered his voice. "You know it's our job to keep you healthy, right?"

"Marines don't need help. We don't give a shit about corpsmen," McClellan replied, dipping his fork full of meatloaf into his gravy.

"Do you want to fight the North Koreans?" Orrin whispered.

"We all do."

"Why are you limping?"

"You gonna turn me in?" McClellan asked, pausing his fork next to his mouth.

"No. This is off the record," Orrin replied.

The proud Marine needed prodding on his pain. McClellan glanced around then took the bite of meatloaf dripping in gravy. He chewed then wiped his chin with the back of his hand.

"I don't want to stay here while my buddies head over," McClellan said.

Orrin nodded. We already knew that. All these guys were gung-ho on killing the North Koreans and Chinese. While McClellan seemed to debate in his head if he could trust a squid, Orrin took a bite of his pasty mashed potatoes. Mine stuck to the roof of my mouth.

"My big toe," McClellan said before downing his glass of powdered milk.

Orrin swallowed his food. "Come over to my bunk tonight and I'll look at it."

"Not at medical?"

"Only if it's serious," Orrin promised.

With a slight nod, Corporal McClellan took his tray of uneaten green beans and left.

"You keep enough confidences, you should be ordained," I said, handing him a dollar.

Orrin smiled and stuffed it into his pocket. "What sins do you have to confess? I know you have some."

"Well, Vicar," I said with a laugh. "My sister makes me tell her everything."

"Everything?" Orrin asked, turning serious. He knocked over his milk reaching for it. He sighed. At least it had spilled onto his tray.

"Everything. I swore I would. Why don't you tell your parents everything?"

"You know why. I don't want to worry my mother," Orrin replied, staring at his liquid dinner.

On the other side of me, Kaminski chimed in. "I don't want to share any of this bullshit so I don't even write home."

"You may change your mind once we get to Korea. If you don't write, they won't write back," Orrin said.

"I'm okay with that. My wife complains in all of hers," Kaminski replied.

As Orrin and I left the mess hall, Sergeant Mayo gave us the stink-eye. Orrin winced, tipping his tray. He rebalanced it and blew out a breath.

"How am I going to carry these monster Marines to safety?" Orrin mumbled.

Later that night in the back corner of our barracks, I watched from the top of my bunk as Orrin packed all his gear into his Marine duffle bag. We had already shipped home our Navy sea bags with Navy uniforms when we first got here. The military thought it helped corpsmen fit in better when wearing Marine dungarees.

We weren't sure what time we'd board the bus for the Naval Air Station's North Island Port, but the higher-ups never told us anything. Since I enlisted in the Navy at the start of the Korean War, that was how it worked. *Learn your damn job, then do your damn job*—one of Sergeant Mayo's favorite sayings.

Orrin stopped when McClellan moseying toward us. The man appeared to ensure his limp didn't show. Orrin pointed to a shadowed part of his bed, away from his letters and toiletries. McClellan sat and gingerly took off his boot and sock. His big toe, red and puffy.

"I told you it was an ingrown toenail," I said, leaning down for a better look. "Marines can't even cut their nails right."

Before McClellan could respond, he winced as Orrin touched his foot. "Will it bench me?"

Orrin shook his head. "First, we soak it. Then, I'll bandage it. Stay here." He returned with hot water in his helmet.

"Did you add magnesium sulfate?" I asked.

"Oh, hell no," McClellan replied. His foot hovered over the water.

"It's just Epsom salt, and yes I did," Orrin said.

McClellan eased his toes into the helmet. Before I could lecture the benefits, Sergeant Mayo stormed into the room. He carried a stack of folded herringbone twill—HBT—uniforms.

"Shit," McClellan whispered.

"Stay put," I said, sliding off my bunk.

Hiding McClellan, Orrin and I stood in front of our beds, the rest of the Marines in front of theirs.

"Armstrong! Connor! Sciulli! Front and center!" Mayo yelled.

After sharing a look, we advanced toward the middle of the room away from McClellan in the shadows still soaking his foot. We stood at attention.

"Where's Sciulli?" Mayo demanded.

"KP again," I replied. Kitchen Police duty was the worst job to have in the military, thus making it every officer's punishment.

"Fine. I'm here to issue Marine uniforms with your FMF insignia. Congratulations, corpsmen." He thrust the folded uniforms at us, then abruptly left.

"How about that?" I said. "We're Fleet Marine Force. I feel dumber already."

The Marines closest narrowed their eyes as Orrin hid his smile.

Orrin checked McClellan's big toe. He dried it, then carefully lifted the corner of the nail and slid a piece of cotton under it. He wrapped it with gauze. "Keep your foot dry. After showering, stuff another piece of cotton under there to keep the pressure off."

McClellan let out his breath and nodded.

"Do us a favor," I said, standing over them. "Cut your nails straight across. Don't curve it. We don't want to see your nasty feet again."

Putting on his sock and boot, McClellan nodded. "Thanks, Squ—Marine," he said before rushing away.

"How is it you're a slob and klutz until your medical training kicks in?" I asked.

Unaffected by the criticism, Orrin shrugged and picked up the helmet. "I don't know."

"Every time you wear that helmet, you're going to smell his stinky foot."

"No, I won't. I used yours," Orrin replied.

I laughed. The war would be bearable with Orrin.

23 November 1952

Dearest Mother and Dad,

Well, training is over. Tomorrow, we ship out. I agree, Dad. My tour in Korea will give me the experience to become a doctor like you. Maybe even working with you at the VA hospital in Amarillo.

Mother, don't worry. Rawley will have my back just like I'll have his. Did you know his grandmother raised him? She's an herbalist. She and Rawley's twin sister run a boarding house with a large garden. They live there, too. He's giving me tips on cultivating the different vegetables. Working in the dirt sounds relaxing. Is that why you enjoy tending to your rose bushes?

Anyway, we head to port early so I'm saying good night. I'm not sure when I'll be able to mail out my letter, but I'll keep writing as long as you write me back. I'll add my new address as soon as I have it.

All the love a son can give,

Orrin

CHAPTER TWO

24 November 1952

Dearest Mother and Dad,

Just a quick note for now. I want to put this in the mail before my adventure begins. It's 0500 and we're on the buses ready to leave for the port. I have a dollar left in American money and I have to get rid of it before we get to Korea so I am enclosing it in this letter.

As a sailor, I'll say we should have fair winds and following seas. Though now I'll need to start thinking like a Marine.

Anyway, I hope you and Dad have a good vacation in Vegas next week. The weather should be nice for you, too. Good luck at the slots, Mother. I'll close for now and write again tomorrow.

All the love a son can give,
Orrin

AS THE BUSES STOPPED IN front of the metal archway of the NAS's North Island Port, the massive transport vessel and attack carrier, U.S.S. *Kearsarge*, greeted us. The beast of a ship, almost three football fields long, already had a major role in the war. Not only did its missions include attacking ground targets, air superiority, and antisubmarine patrols, but it transported Marines—the reason we now boarded the behemoth.

With his Marine duffle bag over his shoulder, Orrin slid his letter into the mailbox at the entrance, then joined me in line with a few other corpsmen. Excitement for an adventure and awe at the huge ship filled the cool, salty air. At least it wasn't raining. We hid our anxiety of going to war. No family or fanfare waited. With hushed voices, the Marines walked toward the ship.

"First to arrive are deeper in the hole," a major yelled at the front of the line.

"Great," I said. "That'll teach us for being on time."

The Marines from George Company snorted. The dozen corpsmen would rotate with them. Sergeant Mayo would be around us much of the time. Oh, boy!

Deep in the bowels of the ship, in a compartment about seventy-five feet wide, the racks four and five bunks high would sleep a total of four hundred men. Mayo pointed to a corner. Orrin set his bag on the bottom and I claimed the one above his. Not much room to move around, if at all. And this was our home for the next week or so.

"All right, thanks for volunteering, squad. We have KP for the next two days. Let's go," Mayo said.

"Don't we get to watch the ship leave port?" Private Alexander Marshall, the injury faker from yesterday, asked.

Orrin and I knew since meeting Marshall that we couldn't compete with him for the ladies. Marshall already had several girlfriends to whom he wrote. They sent him letters with perfumed envelopes. The different scents pressed together left those closest to Marshall lightheaded.

"All your girlfriends meeting in one place to send you off, Private?" Mayo asked, folding his arms.

"No, Sarge!" Marshall replied to the chuckle of those around him.

"We've got three thousand Marines to feed, not to mention all the swabbies running this boat. Move it. Now," Mayo demanded.

Under our breath, we grumbled but followed Mayo to the galley and mess hall. The head cook pointed Orrin, me, Marine Private Jacob Aguilar, and Corpsman Kollen Kunesh to the crates of potatoes.

"Peel," the petite cook said. With anchor tattoos covering his Popeye-like forearms, he pointed to another group. "Wash." Then to another group. "Knead." His one-word demands continued until all the jobs were assigned. No one complained, especially when his thick, meaty hands made fists bigger than heads of cabbage.

I looked at all the potatoes. "We peel all of these?"

"It beats having to touch sticky dough," Aguilar replied, taking the nearby stool.

"I hope that knucklehead Sciulli washes his hands before kneading it," I said, keeping an eye on know-it-all Lukas Sciulli for any shenanigans.

Orrin turned an empty bucket upside-down then promptly landed on the floor beside it. Avoiding eye contact, he climbed onto it and started peeling the mound of potatoes from one of the many crates.

"Aguilar, where you from?" Kollen Kunesh, the overly eager corpsman, asked. "I'm from Manitowoc, Wisconsin."

"Nevada," Aguilar replied.

"Don't ever play him in cards," I said. "They call him *Vegas* for a reason."

Aguilar chuckled. "I want to own a casino someday."

"You got a nickname, Connor," Kunesh asked.

"*Vicar*," I said. "He's good at keeping secrets."

Orrin rolled his eyes. "Sure, and what's yours? *Mouth*?"

"Hey, I like it." With a laugh, I tossed a peeled potato into the dented metal pot.

"I need one," Kunesh said.

"Why?" Orrin asked.

"To fit in," Kunesh replied. "How about *Killer*?"

"You killed someone?" I asked.

Kunesh tossed a potato into the pot with a thud. "Not yet."

"Corpsmen aren't killers," Orrin said. "We protect the injured."

"And kill if necessary." Aguilar threw his into the pot. It missed and bounced on the edge. I caught it before it hit the floor. With a nod of thanks, he continued. "Besides you can't give yourself a nickname. The guys gotta do it."

The head cook came over and looked into the metal pot. "This ain't no quilting bee. You got thirty minutes to peel all those."

"I'm carrying these guys," I said.

"Uh-huh," he replied, unconvinced. "Get to it or you'll be on KP until this war's over."

We glanced at each other, then raced through our crates. The giant pot soon overflowed with peeled tubers. We munched on raw carrots, potatoes, and onions as we worked. It wasn't so bad. We were also the first to taste the rolls right out of the oven. Just the smell made our mouths water. And then with melted butter...oh, boy!

After serving lunch, washing dishes, prepping for dinner, serving it, and then washing those dishes again, Orrin and I treated ourselves to a two-minute shower. We chose the only two freshwater ones. Clueless Marines didn't know they couldn't use regular soap in the saltwater showers. Since regular soap doesn't create a lather in seawater, squids used a special sailor soap. I had a dozen bars to sell and made twenty bucks.

At 2300, we fell into our bunks, too tired to be seasick from the rough waters. Hearing Marines puking, I laughed. It was then I realized it had been Thanksgiving.

At 0400, Sergeant Mayo roused us for another full day of KP. The day was a hot and humid blur. The hole already smelled as if the men hadn't showered in a month. I figured we'd have to get used to the smell at some point. Showers wouldn't be close to the fighting lines.

On the third day, the squad spent as much time as possible topside. We were on the flight deck to view the awe-inspiring, wide-open ocean, but then the fighter jets loudly took off, disturbing our moment of peace. Orrin and I looked for a somewhat quieter place. Orrin wanted to study his first-aid field manual. I wanted to write a letter home.

We walked down the passageway just below the flight deck. The hangar deck took up most of the level except for a room to our right. I opened it, hoping it would be empty. In the big room, one sailor folded canvas and rope, taking up much of the long, waist-high table. He paid us no attention until I cleared my throat. It seemed I'd startled him. He winced then looked over at us.

I glanced at the name on his shirt. "Can we sit in here?"

LeRoy Thompson shook his head and sighed. "I need to concentrate," he said, unfolding the canvas.

"What are you doing?" Orrin asked.

"I'm a parachute rigger," he said as he continued to open the canvas and ropes. "These flyers need me to focus on prepping their chutes. I pray they don't need them, but I give them comfort that they're packed with care if they do."

"An extremely important job," Orrin said. We backed out of the room. Thompson was already ignoring us as he focused back on the unpacked parachute to start again, uninterrupted.

In the hangar deck along the perimeter, Orrin and I walked toward the corner, away from the stored F-2 Banshee and Grumman Panther jets. He sat on a stool. I joined him and we leaned back against the metal bulkhead. Although the sound of the jets leaving the flight deck had decreased in here, we still felt the vibrations through our backs.

I rubbed my nose at the smell of engine oil and spilled fuel in the cooler area. The open side elevator doors, which lifted and lowered the jets, brought in the ocean breeze. A nice change from the humid swamp down below. Twenty sailors ignored us and focused on their jobs with extreme precision.

As Orrin flipped to the chapter about proper ways to carry the wounded, Alexander Marshall walked toward us. I swallowed my annoyance that the guy looked like Cary Grant.

With his box of stationery, Marshall plopped down on the floor beside us. "Sciulli is the gaseousest guy I've ever met."

Orrin snorted. "Ever since I've known him," he replied, not looking up from his manual.

Marshall pulled out a stack of letters. We could see they all started with *Hey Baby.*

"How do you keep them straight?" Orrin asked, glancing at him.

Marshall shrugged. "I don't have to. It's the exact same letter. Saves time."

We nodded like we understood his dilemma of having too many girlfriends. Although Orrin and I wrote to a couple of gals back home and liked receiving their letters, Marshall wrote to eighteen.

Suddenly, we heard a crash, followed by a scream. More shouting followed. Orrin jumped up and ran at the commotion, Marshall and I behind him.

The strap securing a Banshee jet had shifted and snapped from the pressure. The metal hook at the end had hurled across the deck, impaling Petty Officer George Fullaire in the chest. He'd slammed to the ground. A seaman next to Fullaire started to pull out the hook.

"Don't touch it!" Orrin knelt beside the unconscious man whom we had met in the chow line our first day aboard. I could see Orrin quickly assessing the situation. The group hovered, silent. Orrin pointed to the nearest guy in a white T-shirt and Navy bellbottom pants. "Give me your shirt."

He took it off and handed it to Orrin, who packed it around the hook.

"Marshall, go get the Chief Medical Officer. Rawley, get me a litter."

With a nod, Marshall raced away. I grabbed the litter for emergencies that was leaning against the wall. Without being asked, others handed Orrin their white shirts to pack and secure the hook near the man's heart.

Fullaire opened his eyes and tried to move.

"Hold him still," Orrin mouthed to those beside him. With a calm voice, he leaned over his patient. "Fullaire, look at me. You're going to be fine. Tell me your first name," he requested, even though we all knew it.

"George," he replied with tears in his eyes.

"Where you from?" Orrin asked, keeping the pressure around the metal holding it in place.

"Atlanta," he whispered.

His replies let us know his lungs weren't affected. Sweating, George paled but remained conscious. The Chief Medical Officer, Dr. Eggert, and Senior Chief Corpsman Bonner strode toward them.

"Make a hole," Dr. Eggert commanded. Fit and rigid, he parted the men like Moses to the Red Sea.

Pushing his half-moon glasses up the bridge of his nose, Bonner leaned over them and barked, "Litter!"

Marshall and I held it at the ready. Eggert gestured with his hand for us to place Fullaire on it. Orrin supported the hook with bloody hands and walked with the litter toward sickbay.

"Jones! Take everyone's statement. I want to know how this happened," Eggert said, following the group away from the crowd. In a sickbay treatment room, Eggert washed, then gowned up. I observed the immaculate room.

"If I don't make it," Fullaire whispered, "don't let Lizzy see my girlfriend's letters."

"Lizzy's your wife?" Orrin asked.

He nodded. "And there's money in my sea bag to send her. Tell her I love her and I'm sorry."

"You can tell her yourself."

"But if I don't make it—"

With his hands still pressing on the bloody shirts, Orrin calmly reassured Fullaire while Bonner put him under. Once Eggert was ready, Bonner motioned for Orrin to monitor his gas mask so he could assist the doctor.

Looking exhausted, Orrin returned to his bunk. I had put his first-aid field manual and an apple on his bunk. Having missed dinner, he bit into the apple.

"How's he doing?" I asked, leaning over my bunk to look at him.

"The hook missed his lung and heart, but nicked his stomach."

"So liquid diet?"

Orrin nodded as he finished off the apple, core and all. Within a blink of an eye, Sergeant Mayo abruptly stood before us. Orrin and I tensed.

"You both are assigned to sickbay for the duration of our trip. There may be hope for you yet, Connor," Mayo said, before he turned on his heel.

Watching him walk away, Orrin smiled. "That's the nicest thing he's ever said to me."

The next day, Orrin sat beside Fullaire in recovery with two Marines who were incapacitated by severe seasickness. He took Fullaire's vitals while I updated the Marines' paperwork.

"How are you today?" I overheard Orrin asking Fullaire.

"The doc said I'll be fine."

"That's great."

"Uh, so, about what I said before," he said, looking sheepish.

Orrin stopped him. "They call me the *Vicar* for a reason. I can keep a secret. Get some rest and I'll check on you later."

Grimacing, I watched Private Nickolas Bradley dry heave into a bedpan. Bradley lay back and mumbled The Lord's Prayer. The Marines referred to him as "St. Nick", a religious man with his bible in his breast pocket. His thick black hair made him seem more sinister than genial. I was warned not to ask his religious affiliation unless I wanted a long, boring sermon. I didn't like Pastor Mike's homily on Easter Sunday, so I doubted I'd enjoy Bradley's.

Corporal Jack "Tank" DeVos groaned from the next bed. DeVos, a rock-solid Marine, took up the whole bed, with parts of him hanging over the side. Definitely a mean fighting machine.

"Shut the hell up," DeVos said. "Keep your damn praying to yourself."

"Stop swearing, then," Bradley snapped back.

Orrin brought them water and soda crackers. It distracted them, for now. At a table in the corner away from the infirm, Orrin sat down beside me. With his mug of coffee, Dr. Eggert joined us.

"Ready for combat?" Eggert asked.

"We hope so. Any advice?" Orrin asked. We wanted to add to our medical skills.

"There are a few things they probably didn't teach you in school about being in combat. First, remember your sleeping bag has a panic zipper. If you pull it clear up, the bag will fall apart."

We sat up straighter and paid attention.

"Second," Eggert continued, "sleep in your clothes and boots."

"Number three," Bonner added, from the doorway of the pharmacy. "Sleep with your weapon loaded on safe."

Eggert nodded. "Four, sleep with your K-bar or bayonet nearby. And, finally the most important: stay alive to help those who are wounded."

We nodded.

27 November 1952

Dearest Mother and Dad,

Happy Belated Thanksgiving. Chow was pretty good on the ship. I had an extra helping of turkey and gravy but skipped the mashed potatoes though. They didn't look good to me.

Our cruise vacation is going well. All we do is lounge around and eat. On the nice days, we tan topside. These boys really watch out for each other. Why, just yesterday a bunch of men chipped in and helped a swabbie named George Fullaire. Marines and sailors working together? It actually happened.

I assisted in a minor surgery and I learned so much. We received some important advice from the doctor here. I think it will serve us well. In a few more days, we'll land at Inchon. I guess we'll get to Korea about the same time as Ike. I hope he can do some good.

Well, Mother, I had better close for now and I'll write again as soon as I am sure of my new address. In the meantime, keep writing to the same address. It will find me ... eventually.

All the love a son can give,

Orrin

CHAPTER THREE

5 December 1952

Dearest Mother and Dad,

We're in the Yellow Sea almost to Inchon. I'm all packed and ready to go. The weather is getting colder. Rawley said Lake Michigan has waves but not nearly as high or rambunctious as the Pacific. One Marine said it was God's Almighty Power. I agree. It's quite beautiful. It snowed on the ship this morning. I bet I will see some on shore, too.

I read that London had a killer fog making thousands sick. One of our doctors thinks the burning of coal created sulfuric acid particles and that formed sulfur dioxide. A sad turn of events. Dad, since you love chemistry, do you think that's what happened?

Well, we're meeting more and more of the Marines from George Company. The U.S.S. Kearsarge is a huge ship and our living quarters are slightly smaller. We stay out of the way of the seamen prepping the jets that support the boys already fighting.

I hope to get a letter from you once we land. I want to hear about your trip to Vegas. How'd Dad do at the craps table? I will write more later.

All the love a son can give,

Orrin

SINCE LANDING, OUR AFTERNOON WAS made up of lines—lines to exit the ship, lines to load onto the trucks, and lines of trucks to a camp ten miles outside Inchon near Seoul.

Bouncing in the back of a military "cattle" truck next to the back canvas flap, I watched as Orrin peeked out. Although snowless, it was too cold for a dustup from the dirt road. The drab overcast day against the barren, bombed-out land was uninviting. Were we welcome here? Well, we had a job to do. The sooner it got done, the sooner we could go home.

The sergeant who greeted the trucks pointed to the back of another line, the head of which entered a large green canvas tent, hopefully a warm one. Carrying our bags and equipment, our group joined the line and bobbed in place to keep warm. Sometime that day, we would find out our assignments. Would the corpsmen head to the rear Battalion Reserve hospital nearby, to a Medical Evacuation hospital close to the front, to a Forward Aid Station just behind the fighting, or on patrol with the Marines on the frontlines?

"I want on the lines first thing," Lukas Sciulli said, breaking the silence. I sneered at the irritating vibrato in his voice.

Since Camp Pendleton, Sciulli rubbed me the wrong way with his ambitious ass-kissing to all the officers. He had messed up my bunk right before inspection. He said it was an accident but I thought otherwise. Sciulli's bunk by comparison looked neater. Both bunks still looked better than Orrin's.

"I'd prefer to ease into it," I replied.

"I'm not scared," Sciulli said.

I clenched my jaw and turned away. The knucklehead was right; I was scared. I don't want to die. To show my anxiety though was a sign of weakness. Never again in front of anyone.

Inching forward with the men, Orrin remained quiet. I knew he'd save any consoling for those wounded in the fight.

The tent looked chaotic inside, but it was actually well-organized. Stopping at each table, the corpsmen received our 782 Gear named after the DD form we had to sign. It consisted of the supplies for our medical bags, ammo for our weapons, cold weather boots, two wool blankets to go with our sleeping bags, and a few other items. After switching boots, we lugged all our gear to the next tent for chow of coffee and soup, both thankfully hot. The women servers greeted us with big smiles and friendly encouragement. I couldn't help but smile back as I nudged Orrin and his goofy grin down the line. Orrin tripped but quickly recovered.

Finding a vacant spot at the end of a long table, I sat and downed my chicken noodle soup. The salty warmth soothed me.

"Efficient, I'd say," Sciulli said, sitting across from Orrin and me. He seemed to follow us around like a lost puppy. It annoyed me. At least puppies were cute.

"They've been doing this for over a year," I replied, scowling. "They better be efficient by now."

As soon as the wandering sergeant saw our empty soup bowls, he pointed us to a line for the next tent. I stood in front of a clean-cut lieutenant behind a table. He seemed bored. I would be too, if this was my job during the war. Safe and tedious.

"Name," he asked, not looking up from the thick stack of pages in front of him.

"Corpsman 3rd Class Rawley Armstrong."

He flipped through the pages on his clipboard. "First Marines, Third Battalion, George Company, Able Med Station. Next!"

That meant I would support the Marines of George Company at their evacuation hospital close to the front, but not on it. I followed the line out of that tent. Those in front of me headed for the last cluster of tents where we'd sack out for the night. I waited to see where my buddy was going. Would it be time to say goodbye? Would I ever see Orrin again?

Smiling, Orrin stopped next to me. "Same," he said. "This war might not be so bad."

I nodded, elated by the news.

"Hey, I'm at Able Med, too," Sciulli shouted as he left the tent. I swore under my breath.

Up at 0500, the sergeants rushed us to chow and then to the trucks again. Those of us heading closer to the front boarded the troop train. The rest went to the reserves nearby.

Like sardines packed in a can, Marines squeezed in everywhere. On the benches and on the floor, George Company men and their gear. Across the aisle, Jacob

"Vegas" Aguilar tried to get a craps game started. Sergeant Mayo slept with one eye open, preventing anyone from joining in.

Most Marines slept, lulled by the rocking rails, the chugging engine, and the heat from all the bodies. Leaning against a propped blanket on the window, Orrin appeared to fade in and out. He said he'd write a letter home later when he had more privacy. I stared out the window at the war-barren land in winter. Nothing lived. I shuddered.

Brian McClellan pointed to his foot and gave us a thumb's up. Orrin nodded. We knew some of these men already. Feeling better after a week's worth of seasickness, Nickolas "St. Nick" Bradley and Jack "Tank" DeVos chatted and showed each other pictures of their families back home. Alexander "Hey Baby" Marshall wrote his letters while Dale Kaminski dozed against his nondescript twin McClellan's shoulder. Drool dripped out of Kaminski's mouth onto McClellan's arm, creating a stream of slime. I doubted it would be the most disgusting thing I saw over here. But it was still gross.

Five hours later, we stopped at a three-tent encampment. A dozen trucks and two Flying Medivacs waited. A sergeant pointed the three corpsmen to a helicopter. Luckily, the Sikorski had enough room inside with the mounted litters for the wounded, not the choppers with the exposed exterior litters. That would have been a cold ride. The three corpsmen would settle in at Able Med while the Marines from George Company set up somewhere behind the MLR (Main Line of Resistance).

Instead of yelling over the loud engine, we gazed out the windows at the paddy fields framed by pathetic-looking dirt roads. The huts still standing were abandoned or in need of patching.

Able Med was an evacuation hospital made up of large corrugated metal buildings for surgery and recovery, green canvas tents for living quarters, and a number of sandbag bunkers for emergencies.

All to be broken down and moved to a new site at a moment's notice—well, a few hours' notice. I had heard earlier in the war, Evac hospitals moved every few days. Not so much now. What a pain in the ass that must have been!

Two men met us at the chopper landing pad on top of a small hill. Colonel Caleb Levitt, the commanding officer, shook our hands. Short in stature, he was pleasant.

"Ringer will get you settled. He has the daily roster of your duties," Levitt said, before leaving with our assignment papers.

Orrin stepped forward to shake Ringer's hand. In his mid-twenties, the corpsman with big ears and a big nose pumped his hand once then turned toward the cluster of canvas tents just below the landing pad. We followed with all our gear.

"Corpsmen are divided up in the two tents. This one's yours," he said, opening the tent's thin wooden door. "Some are on duty in the recovery wards and some are on the line."

"Where you from?" Sciulli asked.

"It doesn't matter. Do your best and we won't have a problem," Ringer said, motioning for us to enter.

Two corpsmen lay across their bunks writing letters. They sat up as Ringer introduced them.

"That's Joe Garcia," Ringer said, pointing to the man on the left. "And that's Petey Parsons." He abruptly turned and exited the tent.

"They call me *Red*," Parsons said, tapping his bright red hair. His freckles covered his face and neck. "Don't mind Ringer. He's been here the longest and stopped making friends with the corpsmen three deaths ago. A lot of turnover."

Orrin and I exchanged a look. Sciulli swallowed.

Welcome to Able Med.

8 December 1952

Dearest Mother and Dad,

We made it to Able Med, which is ten miles behind the line and about forty miles north of Seoul. Dad, I know you've heard of M.A.S.H. units (Mobile Army Surgical Hospitals). They're for the Army. Well, our Able Med Evac Hospital is similar but specifically for the Marines.

Having a hospital closer to the front—not on it—is the best thing for the wounded. We can help them quickly and save the lives of so many.

We sleep in squad tents set up for ten corpsmen in each. I've met the corpsmen in ours and will meet the rest soon. Our shifts and assignments are always changing. We do all types of jobs here from cleaning bedpans in the recovery wards to assisting in surgeries.

Our medical supplies are always with us so we can hold "sick call" for the men, who have colds, cuts, or other minor injuries. They seek us out in secret so not to ruin their reputations as tough fighting Marines.

Anyway, our oil stove will keep us warm as the temperature starts to drop. Our mail has been trailing us so I'm hoping to get one from you tomorrow. Please use my new address. Your letters will find me quicker.

All the love a son can give,

Orrin

CHAPTER FOUR

16 December 1952

Dearest Mother and Dad,

I finally received a letter from you. The mail has had a hard time finding us. Mother, I wish you would write as often as you could. I know you worry, but you shouldn't. They say we'll rotate enough from the front to the reserves in the rear so I'll avoid any danger.

I can tell you everything over here is a lot better than I had ever thought could be. We don't have to pitch tents and we get all the chow we want. So, it isn't at all bad. I'm going to watch all the minor surgeries I can for the experience since there doesn't seem to be much going on right now. I guess the cold weather has slowed down the fighting and will slow it down even more if the weather gets worse.

The men are finding a variety of ways to stay busy. Most are writing home. Some bet on just about everything, mostly to brag about winning. Our C.O. doesn't allow us to bet with money.

All the love a son can give,

Orrin

AFTER TOSSING OUR SCRUBS IN the bin outside the six-table operating room, Orrin and I dressed and threw on our winter coats. We needed some fresh air. Watching Dr. James operate on a Marine with appendicitis fascinated us. A nice, neat, clean procedure. Although Major Michael James had only a week's training in combat, he was an excellent doctor and teacher.

As we stopped outside the door, Kim, a ten-year-old Korean boy, and Sciulli raced down the snow-covered road on sleds made from the metal lids of the trash cans. Lining the road from the chopper pad at the top of the hill to the mess tent below, Marines cheered them on as they zipped past.

At the bottom of the hill, Sciulli and Kim dug their heels in the snow to slow down. Out of control, Sciulli crashed into Major Gordon Daniels, a self-described God-like doctor, stepping out of the mess. He knocked Daniels onto his back. The Marines along the road scattered quickly, finding something else to do. Daniels lay sprawled out in the doorway. Still sitting on the lid, Kim gaped wide-eyed at Sciulli, who had taken out the two trash cans, spreading leftover biscuits and gravy over him and the area.

Major Daniels geared up to yell but stopped and stared at the boy. He lifted the boy's winter cap, felt his head, and then inspected his face, neck, and arms.

"I want this boy quarantined and tested," he said to Sciulli.

"Why?" Sciulli asked.

"I think he has smallpox."

The men standing in the mess to watch the drama took two steps back. Too late.

"Connor!" Daniels yelled. "Call headquarters for vaccine. We'll need to inoculate everyone."

"Yes sir," Orrin replied.

I tagged along to the office and listened to the frustrating bureaucracy. Transferred to four different people outranking the one before, Orrin remained on the line for forty-five minutes.

Major Daniels stood in the doorway. "Is it on the way?"

"Not yet, sir," Orrin replied. "They don't believe me."

"Give me that," he said, grabbing the phone. "Go find out from that dumbass Sciulli the places that kid has been."

Orrin nodded and turned on his heel. I would've loved to see Sciulli get chewed out if it weren't for everyone having to get an injection. We waited outside the small canvas tent set up away from the others. Inside, Sciulli raised the window flap on the wooden door.

"He's been all over camp, right?" Orrin asked.

Dejected, Sciulli nodded. "We've been using Kim as a translator with the villagers down the road."

"Stay put with the boy until we have the vaccine," Orrin replied.

"How the hell did you let this happen?" I demanded.

"I don't know," Sciulli mumbled.

"The whole 1st Marine Division needs to be vaccinated as well as the locals," I said.

"It's not really his fault," Orrin replied. "Not like he gave Kim smallpox."

"No," Colonel Levitt, our C.O., said behind us. "But he should have noticed it sooner."

"Sorry, sir," Sciulli said. He turned away and wiped his face.

Levitt ignored him. "Connor, you and Armstrong set up a couple of tables in recovery then get everyone lined up. The vaccine's being flown in."

Able Med became the hub for the Marines on their way to the front and for those coming back. There hadn't been any engagements so the Marines returning from their patrol on the MLR were just tired, cold, and dirty.

After he tested clean, Sciulli carried a tray of mugs with hot coffee and handed them out to the Marines in line. He had grunt duty and gladly did all the shit jobs with the promise that Able Med not tell the Marines he was the reason they needed inoculations.

Orrin and I greeted the Marines in the two screened areas for semi-privacy. As we vaccinated the men, we learned as many of their names as we could. Orrin had said it was important for their morale. It helped that they talked about home, which gave us context to remember them by.

After hitting the chow line, the Marines coming off the MLR formed another line for shots. It took us a little longer as we tended to minor injuries—scrapes, scratches, and blisters on hands and feet. A few had the makings of frostbite on their toes.

Orrin smiled at Alexander Marshall next in line. "Hey Baby, how are you?"

Always clean-shaven even in the field, Marshall snorted at his nickname.

"Are you getting letters back from the ladies?" Orrin asked, jabbing him with a needle.

"Not yet. I heard a truck's bringing in a big bag of mail," he replied as he rolled down his sleeve.

Next, Orrin nervously waved in short and stocky Sergeant Mayo. "Hey, Sarge."

Mayo hopped onto the table, baring his arm for the shot. "Whose fault is this?"

Not wanting to answer, Orrin drew the serum. "Any injuries you want me to look at?"

"I'm guessing Sciulli, right? It's just the boneheaded thing he'd do."

Overhearing them, I coughed, confirming Mayo's guess. After his shot, Mayo left in a huff. I hoped Sciulli stunk at hide and seek.

Jacob Aguilar a.k.a. "Vegas" dropped his coat in a chair and rolled up his sleeve. Orrin liked him mostly because Aguilar was shorter than Orrin was.

"Hey Vicar, still keeping secrets?" Aguilar asked.

"Of course, Vegas," Orrin replied, standing up straighter to tower over him by two full inches. "You need me to take your confession?"

He laughed. "Not me. I'm a choir boy."

"With a pocket full of cash?" Orrin asked.

Smiling, Vegas nodded and lowered his voice so the other Marines couldn't hear. "I send it all to my grandma to help take care of Grandpa who lost his arm in WWI."

Orrin gave him the shot then patted him on the head. "Go with God, my son."

With a laugh, Vegas put on his coat as he left. To the next Marine, he said, "The vicar will see you now."

Wearing a big crucifix around his neck with his dog tags, Nickolas "St. Nick" Bradley entered Orrin's side of the half-screened area. With black hair and dark stubble, he still looked disturbing to me. I was sure he had sinful secrets.

"You're a vicar?" St. Nick asked.

"No, I—" Orrin started.

"So you pose as a vicar? That's sacrilegious," he said.

"Of course not. Roll up your sleeve. I listen, is all."

"Oh," he said, sitting on the exam table. "Well, I pray for these men's souls, but they don't appreciate it."

I always thought a good deed such as praying for a soul didn't need recognition.

"They probably do," Orrin replied. "They just don't say it out loud. A bunch of tough guys."

Apparently happy to be recognized for his benevolent thoughts, St. Nick moved on. Orrin and I continued throughout the afternoon and evening. When we thought we were done, another squad arrived. Sciulli brought us sandwiches and more medical supplies.

A few Korean families from the local village came in for a meal and a vaccination. A very pregnant woman and her husband entered my area. All of a sudden, there was a splash. I swore.

"You okay over there?" Orrin asked.

"No. This woman's water just broke," I replied.

"Sciulli, find one of the doctors and get her to the O.R.," Orrin said.

Wide-eyed, Sciulli slipped in the puddle, used the table to recover, then helped the woman out the door. I quickly cleaned the mess as the husband gaped at us, looking scared. Dr. James came through the area and pointed the soon-to-be father to a different area to wait.

After we injected five more Koreans and eight Marines, Orrin waved in his last patient. Jack "Tank" DeVos already had his sleeve rolled up while I put my equipment away and straightened my area. His jaw clenched, brows furrowed. Setting his carbine and coat on the chair, he plopped onto the exam table, which seemed to sag under his sturdy weight.

"How you doing, Tank?" Orrin asked.

"I'm angry," he replied.

Orrin nodded as if he knew why. "I heard a rumor that the mail truck is on its way here."

Tank's body immediately relaxed. "Mail? Really?"

Orrin gave him the inoculation. "I haven't gotten any mail lately, either."

"It's the only good thing over here," Tank replied.

"It'll find us. Are you writing home?"

"Not so much. I know I'm a terrible husband and father," he said, slumping his huge shoulders.

"For not writing home? Don't beat yourself up. You've been a little busy. So how old are your kids?"

Tank automatically took out a photo and handed it to him. "Claire's five and Nora's two. That's Jessica, my wife."

"Glad your girls have your wife's good looks," Orrin said, showing the picture to me.

Tank laughed. "Yeah."

Talking about his family eased any tension Tank had. It seemed to make Orrin happy, too. Leaving the ward by 2100, Orrin and I saw Dr. James in the center of the compound.

"How's the baby?" Orrin asked him.

"A girl. So sweet and innocent. The mom's doing well." Bringing life into the world surely caused a good mood. Smiling, James wandered away.

Orrin turned to me as we walked into our tent. "I heard the truck arrived earlier. I sure hope it had mail in it or there'll be a bunch of unhappy Marines."

"And unhappy corpsmen." I looked at Sciulli's bunk next to Orrin's. "Where's that knucklehead?"

Sitting on his cot, Petey "Red" Parsons, on the opposite twelve-hour shift as we were, tightened the laces on his boots. "On the MLR with Sergeant Mayo's squad," he said, slipping on his coat. "Looks like we're starting up again." Parsons mumbled something else.

"What, Red?" Orrin asked. "I didn't hear you."

"Oh, nothing, just a pep talk. It helps me prepare," he said sheepishly as he fumbled with the zipper on his heavy coat.

"That makes sense," Orrin replied, sitting on his bunk. "I'll try that, too."

Red paused for a second before leaving the tent for his shift.

"I heard the fellas teasing him about that," I said. "I think you just validated that his pep talks aren't a sign he's crazy."

I wondered what I should do so that I didn't go crazy.

18 December 1952

Dearest Mother and Dad,

We haven't been very busy. A good thing. We've been taking care of the Korean people mostly. I assisted Dr.

James in some minor surgeries. He removed a cataract from a Korean woman and fixed a cleft lip on a Korean boy.

Mother, I know they do almost anything here at Able Med, but the other day took the cake. We had a Korean woman give birth to a baby girl. I saw her the next day. So tiny.

Well, I'm meeting more and more of the Marines. The corpsmen take good care of them.

I guess you're wondering what to send me for Christmas. The only thing I want is mail from home. That would please me more than anything else you could send.

All the love a son can give,

Orrin

CHAPTER FIVE

20 December 1952

Dearest Mother and Dad,

I'm happy your dinner party was a grand success. Rose and Mitch Kershaw must have been envious that you had Bob Camp play the piano. Did you sing O Come, All Ye Faithful? *You know it's my favorite.*

I'm glad you liked the pictures I sent of me and my buddies. Yes, I do smoke and so do you, Mother. I'm not doing it because everyone else is. Also, Jenny Spicer wrote to me first. I like getting mail so I wrote her back. I am not stringing her along. We're friendly. That's all.

Yes, Mother, I am well aware I have two and a half more years of service to the Navy. I'll stop writing her if that's what you want.

And, yes, I have had a drink since training, but one beer doesn't make me a bum.

My best friend, Rawley, prefers I drive the jeep when we see the sights. How about that? I'm a responsible driver and keep under the speed limit. The rough roads make for slow going anyway.

Rawley and I have been sharing our treats from home so it's like we get double the mail. By the way, I left you each a Christmas gift. You'll find them in the shoe box on the top shelf in my closet. Surprise! Please write as often as you can.

All the love a son can give,

Orrin

DRIVING A JEEP TOWARD A Forward Aid Station, Orrin turned on the heat and swerved slightly. I glared at his speed as usual. I'd drive, but I hated driving a stick shift. I could do it. I just didn't like it.

The heat in the jeep wouldn't work. We had no luck when it came to a workable vehicle. Bundled up with scarves and thin wool caps under our helmets, we still froze without the canvas roof. We had a hard time fitting wounded into the vehicle with one. The more wounded we could transfer, the better.

"I'm not reckless, just cold," Orrin said. He sighed and glanced at me, opening my small package from home. We had mail call at 1800 then Colonel Levitt ordered us to the front to help out. Orrin had mailed out his letter before leaving.

"What did you tell your parents this time? That we're in a resort eating caviar and drinking champagne?" I liked to give him a hard time about lying to them. A sore spot for both of us. About the only thing we disagreed on.

"Yes, and that my best friend's a knucklehead."

"Sciulli's your best friend?"

"No, you are," he replied.

"I am?" I asked.

"Yes. Need a handkerchief?"

"You're mine, too." I smiled and stuffed a cookie into my mouth as we bounced in and out of the potholes on the frozen dirt road. I moaned as the cookie melted against my tongue.

"Where's mine, best friend?" Orrin asked, keeping one eye on the road and the other on the nearby hill.

"So you only love me for my sister's cookies?" I asked, searching the hill, too.

"Yes." Orrin swerved to miss the largest pothole yet. A crater, really.

Close to the fighting, we never knew when a sniper would fire a shot, especially at dusk when vehicles were heading toward the MLR. Snipers wanted to kill the ones trying to help the wounded. The more chaos, the better for the enemy.

"Keep her on the road, please," I said. "Anyone ever tell you that you stink at driving?"

"Everyone," Orrin replied, seeming unaffected by the criticism.

I leaned over with a thick sugar cookie. Keeping both hands on the wheel, Orrin opened his mouth. He groaned, too. "Less sugar and more baking soda," I said. "The way I like them."

Orrin nodded. "Much better than the sweet candies my mother sends me. Not that I'm complaining. While I don't care for them, the men in recovery do."

Turning on the jeep's headlights, Orrin approached Forward Aid, nothing more than a rounded sandbag bunker on the back side of a large hill. Usually the hill the fighting was on.

Wounded Marines received an initial assessment and first aid in the field where a corpsman then sent them to a Forward Aid Station for treatment. From there, they were sent on to Able Med or another Evac hospital for surgery and such.

Orrin and I stopped to find men shouting orders and other men screaming in pain. Flashlight beams moved rapidly around the area like Hollywood spotlights. We jumped from the jeep and immediately headed for the corpsman in charge, Petey Parsons, this time. The young redhead sorted out the chaos with his demands.

"The bus is on the way," I said. "Red, who needs to go now?"

"Any choppers?" Red asked.

"No," Orrin replied. "They're helping Easy Med on Bunker Hill."

With a nod, Red pointed to two Marines on litters. "Chest wound and head wound."

We quickly loaded both unconscious men. One secured on the hood shielded under a blanket and the other across the backseat also covered. Morphine numbed their pain for now. Hopefully it would last through the bumpy ride back to Able Med.

Orrin drove while I pressed the thick bandage on the Marine's chest in the backseat to keep him stabilized. Trying to miss the potholes, Orrin drove as quickly as he could. For once, I didn't mind. We came upon the bus alongside the dirt road. Orrin stopped. A sniper had killed the driver. Someone peeked out the back window. Relieved to see us, the newest corpsman, Gene Eugene, had been hit in the shoulder.

"Rawley, take the jeep. I'll take the bus back to Forward Aid for the others," Orrin said.

I turned to Eugene. "Can you drive?" He nodded. "Take these men to Able Med. I'm going back to Forward, too."

Orrin and I jumped into the bus while Eugene drove the two wounded Marines away in the jeep. Orrin moved the driver aside. Dark blood covered the side window. Hearing a bullet hit the side of the bus, he floored it, hopefully away from the sniper's sights. At the aid station, he backed in and we helped to load the wounded inside. Red raised an eyebrow.

"Sniper," I said.

"That bastard shot out a tire earlier," Red replied, pointing at the disabled jeep. Riding the rim had destroyed it. "I radioed for support. Somebody needs to get off their ass." Red growled and strode toward the next group of wounded Marines coming in. At eighteen, he got worked up like a seasoned vet. Those pep talks of his really worked.

With a full bus, Orrin hurried to the driver's seat. "All right men, hold on! We got a sniper somewhere on the left. Keep your heads down." He stripped the gear. I made sure everyone was strapped in. Near the sniper's perch, he shifted and gunned it.

Corporal George "Biggie" Biggs with a bandage around his calf had his carbine sticking halfway out the broken window. Biggie—really named for his girth and not his last name—hated everyone. He had yet to say something nice to anyone.

"I'll take care of that gook," Biggie said. "It's payback time."

"A sniper by definition means you won't see him, idiot," Jacob "Vegas" Aguilar said. He had a bandage around his head.

"Shut up, you damn Mexican," Biggie said.

"I'm American, you racist shit," Vegas replied.

St. Nick, with a shoulder wound, added his religious two cents' worth. "God loves all his creatures."

"Did you just call me a *creature*?" Biggie demanded.

Before the argument escalated, the bus took two shots from the sniper. Suddenly, mortars bombarded the crest of the hill, lighting up the area. Orrin blew out a breath and kept driving. A few conscious cheered. Petey Parsons, the red-headed warrior, came through for them.

At Able Med, the other corpsmen waited for Orrin to completely stop the bus, then they hurried to unload and prioritize the wounded. Colonel Levitt, their commanding officer, stopped us from stepping down.

"We've got more at the aid station," Levitt said, blocking the doorway.

Hearing the backdoor slam shut, Orrin started the empty bus again and peeled out, speeding away. Hanging on tight, I stood beside him.

"This new bullet hole is two inches from your head," I said.

"I don't want to think about it."

The burning fire on the crest gave us a brief reprieve until the next sniper took his perch somewhere else along the road.

"I could use another cookie," Orrin said, bouncing in his seat.

"Damn! I left my box in the jeep." I plopped down on the bench that secured the litters in place, two tiers holding twelve litters total.

With eight more wounded, we raced back to Able Med. Rubbing his butt, Orrin stepped down as Major James yelled for him to find the Korean interpreter.

"There's a Korean woman shot and in labor. She's in x-ray," James said.

Orrin grabbed Kim, the young boy, from the mess tent and rushed him to x-ray—just in time for Kim to translate "twins". Orrin tended to her shoulder wound as I assisted Major James. Translating for the doctor, Kim helped coach her through labor. Her husband was nowhere in sight. Having a bowling ball come out your cha-cha? Twice?

Yikes! I imagined the woman barely felt Orrin take out the bullet and stitch her up.

The wounded Marines slept in the two recovery wards. Screened off for privacy, the mom and twin boys also slept, for now. Orrin and I checked the men's vitals and marked their charts.

"Vicar," Private Lesley Wright whispered. The rugged Marine had been shot in the stomach. No artery had been hit. Most likely, he'd rehab for a while.

Orrin walked over and sat on a stool beside him. "You should be sleeping."

"I gotta know. Am I going home?"

"I don't know. I'm not the doctor," Orrin replied. Even if we knew the answer, we would never say. Orrin and I had agreed back at Fort Sam Houston. Let the doctors be hated if the wounded Marines had to stay and fight. "I'd send everyone home if given the chance. You got a sweetie waiting for you?" Orrin asked.

"Not anymore," he replied, clenching his jaw.

"Sorry," Orrin said. "Do you want to talk about it?"

Wright shook his head but started talking anyway. "She dumped me for my best friend. When I get home, I'm killing that no-good, dirty dentist. She married him for the money. I can't believe I fell for her innocent act."

"You know if you kill him, you'll be thrown into the brig. She must really be worth it," Orrin replied.

Wright opened his mouth for a second before he spoke. "She'd enjoy bragging about that. What do you think I should do?"

Orrin thought for a moment. "Find someone who makes you happy."

Wright laughed. "She'd hate that."

At 0800, Corpsmen Lukas Sciulli and Gerry Goodman, a nice enough guy, came to relieve us. Goodman was always hot. Not with a fever, just a higher than average body temperature. He rarely wore his winter coat.

"Any problems?" Goodman asked.

"No," Orrin said. "When they wake up, keep Biggs away from Aguilar. They may get into a fistfight if you don't."

We hit the tepid showers then slid into our sleeping bags. Orrin had two blankets on top of him. The only thing he ever complained about was that he was cold.

That afternoon, I heard Orrin's growling stomach and smiled. The delicious smell of my spices made him sit up. I stirred the metal pot on our oil stove. Sciulli tried to dip in his finger for a taste, but I slapped his hand.

"Wait your turn," I told him.

"What'd you make?" Orrin asked.

"I turned our c-rations into chili. I mixed in pork and beans, a can of sausage patties, and some herbs from home." I savored a spoonful and nodded. The corpsmen dashed to form a line with their metal bowls from their mess kits.

Orrin joined them and took a big bite. "This is the best chili I've ever had and I'm from Texas," he said, closing his eyes. "What a delicious Christmas gift."

24 December 1952

Dearest Mother and Dad,

Merry Christmas! Although by the time you get this, it'll be 1953 so Happy New Year. There isn't anything to do here at Able Med except sit around, play cards, and listen to the radio so I volunteered to drive the bus around for those that need to go places. It keeps my boredom in check.

From here, you hardly even know there's a war going on. We sure are lucky to have all the air power over Korea. The 11th Marines and their artillery are pretty great, too. They took out a sniper before he could cause a problem.

We had a Korean woman in labor. Without anything else to do, Dr. James wanted us to x-ray her as a precaution. She had twins. The father was shocked and not so happy.

As an early Christmas gift, Rawley made us chili from the herbs his sister sent him. For our dessert, I shared your sweets. Some of the other corpsmen shared their treats from home, too. We had quite a celebration.

Enclosed is my pay to put into my savings account. I think it will be pretty hefty by the time I get home. That's all for now.

All the love a son can give,

Orrin

CHAPTER SIX

25 December 1952

Dearest Mother and Dad,

Well, this is my second Christmas away from you both. And the second time I will miss seeing Dad dressed as Santa at the VA hospital. I hope you send me pictures. I'm glad you make it a special time for the vets. They deserve it.

I'm not sure when I'll be home. Since I'm stationed close but not on the frontlines, I will only be here nine months then I'll return to the States to finish my commitment to the Navy.

Mother, I'm sorry I won't be able to get you a gift from Japan until I go on leave there. I don't know when that'll be. I'm sure it won't be for a while. I'll find you the perfect present though.

I'll write more later. We're going to watch The Yankee Buccaneer. *The first movie we've seen since we got here. It will give us a break from the boredom.*

All the love a son can give,

Orrin

EXCITEMENT FILLED THE CROWDED MESS tent as Orrin found his saved seat in the second row. He handed me one of the two mugs of coffee, then sipped his.

"I wish this was popcorn," I said.

"Me, too," Orrin replied.

We were still full from Christmas chow but popcorn would have hit the spot. With the movie, we were finally getting a break from our reality. The lights turned off. The crowd hushed. The music started. The opening credits scrolled. The air raid siren screamed. The men groaned.

"Flash Red!" someone shouted.

The projector stopped and men ran from the mess tent. After practicing this drill many times, we knew our assignments. Turning on our flashlights, Orrin and I headed for the recovery ward.

Sciulli shined a light in our faces. "What's going on?"

"Enemy planes nearby," Orrin said, holding up his hand to block the light.

"Wounded go into the bunker," I said. "Grab a litter."

The ones who could walk followed Sciulli and me carrying the heavyweight Biggs on a litter. Orrin and Goodman moved Wright to one and then to the bunker with the rest. Inside, the wounded men crowded into the nine bunks, three beds high. Comfort was nil. The cold space quickly heated with all the bodies inside and so did the horrid smell of body odor. We breathed from our mouths.

"Would the enemy really bomb a field hospital?" Vegas asked, rubbing the gauze around his temple.

"Hell yeah," Biggie said loudly. "Those no-good dirty gooks. I don't know why the hell we're here. My dad died on Okinawa. I say blast all these heathens to hell so we can go home." On a roll, Biggs looked at Vegas. "As bad as those Mexican bastards invading our country from the south."

Vegas started swearing back at Biggie. That fired up St. Nick, who spouted bible verses about loving thy neighbor.

"Everyone, shut the hell up," I yelled. "If any of you knuckleheads reinjure your wounds, I'm going to sew you to each other!"

Someone in the back laughed, releasing the tension. Orrin dug into the bottom of his medical bag and pulled out a small round tin. He gave it to me.

"Who wants fudge?" I asked with a smile. After passing out the sweets, I handed the empty tin back to Orrin.

"You can't argue if your mouth's full," Orrin said.

Leaving the vulgar quarreling and rotten funk, Orrin and I held our carbines outside the bunker door. We watched Frisco Hill and heard the thunderous bombing. Around 0200, the injured Marines returned to their ward and Orrin and I made our way to the beds with the other corpsmen.

The P.A. System had other ideas. "Incoming wounded. All shifts report."

While the three other corpsmen were already on duty, the remaining seven in our tent moaned as one and set out for the chaos to begin again.

To make room for the newly wounded, Orrin and I loaded the ones already in the ward onto the bus where they would go to the Battalion Reserve hospital near Seoul. From there, the Marines would be reassessed and sent back to the lines or shipped home.

"I don't want to see you bums again," I said.

"We don't want to see you again, either," Wright said. "And thanks."

"Do me a favor. No talking on the bus. Let the driver drive," Orrin said.

Biggie nodded. "He's not a darky so I'm good."

Orrin walked away as the arguing revved up again. For some, the depression set in no matter which direction they were heading. Those Marines shipped home worried about their buddies still here and what the future held once home. Those returning to the MLR worried about their recent trauma. Would it hinder them from having their brothers' backs? Would it get them injured again? Or worse, killed? Would knowing the outcome be better? Of all the Marines Orrin and I chatted with, none had an answer.

"Connor, Armstrong," Major Levitt commanded. "Dr. James wants you to assist him."

"Yes sir," we replied.

The operating room was already busy as we scrubbed up. I turned to Orrin. "We've met a lot of Marines from George Company. How am I going to feel if, at some point, we work on someone we know?" I asked. It had been bothering me for a while now.

Orrin hesitated. I caught his pained look just before he seemed to mask it. "We've already worked on Marines we know, right?" he said.

"Minor injuries, not life-threatening ones."

"I don't know. I guess we focus on the task at hand." Orrin didn't sound all that convincing. I hoped I could keep it together.

We approached the last surgery table. Brian McClellan, the Marine who had the ingrown toenail, had his chest cracked open. His heart still. Staring, Orrin swallowed hard and stood emotionless beside the tray of surgical instruments. He glanced at me with wide eyes. I wanted to mouth, "Focus," but my mask wouldn't allow it.

"His heart stopped so we haven't much time," Dr. James said. Elbow deep, his bloody gloved hand squeezed the heart.

I wondered how doctors could remain unaffected. Was there special training for that? You'd think we'd have a course on it. I did what Orrin said and focused. Orrin, on autopilot, handed Dr. James the tools he needed. Time stood still. I had brought up the question earlier more for me, but Orrin seemed to have a worse time. I wished he'd talk to me.

That night, I suspected more horrors of war invaded Orrin's dreams. My best friend tossed and turned. Gasping for a breath, Orrin jolted awake. From the bunk above, I looked down at him. He rubbed the wetness from his eyes.

"You okay?" I whispered.

"No," he replied, turning away.

Only in the middle of the night could Orrin be honest with me.

28 December 1952

Dearest Mother and Dad,

Miracles do happen over here. I saw something that very few people ever see. A Marine's heart stopped and the doctor went in and started it beating again with his hand. The man was dead for two minutes but the doctor brought him back to life.

Unfortunately, McClellan lived for only seventy-two hours before his other body systems shut down. The fact that his heart stopped and then started again is amazing. I just wish the outcome would have been different. He was a good Marine.

On a lighter note, How Company put on quite a show in front of us—like New Year's Eve fireworks. What a way to celebrate! I pray the new year brings us hope for the future and one step closer to when we all can go home.

I'm hitting the sack now so I'll write more soon.

All the love a son can give,

Orrin

CHAPTER SEVEN

31 December 1952

Dearest Mother and Dad,

I hope you have fun cutting a rug at Antonia David's New Year's Eve party. I have a feeling we'll ring in the New Year's Day with a few rounds of artillery, just for fun.

Thank you for the wool socks and brownies. I shared the sweets with the men in the recovery ward. They loved them. You really made their day better. I've become protective of the men here. Who knew a squid would care about Marines? Believe it or not, they take care of us, too.

Here's more of my pay to add to my savings. The big discussion around here is which model car is the best. It will be the first thing I buy when I get home. Well, we don't have to worry too much about the cold weather because we have plenty of warm clothes and layers. I'll write more later.

All the love a son can give,

Orrin

AT DUSK, ORRIN DROVE THE jeep on the way to the MLR. He and I would meet up with the Marines who have been sleeping, eating, and fighting on a hill they called Reno. We sweated in our fatigues, winter coats, vests, three bandoliers of supplies, our medical knapsacks, ammo belts, and carbines.

"How are we supposed to move quickly with all this gear weighing us down?" I asked.

"We're warm," Orrin replied, shrugging.

The hill wasn't a casual slope of tall green grass like the ones at home. The Korean hills had jagged, protruding rock formations with narrow ridges at the top and clusters of leafless bushes throughout the area. The trees had been blown to bits long ago. We headed to the outpost just below the top along the sub-ridges. Tonight, we supported the Marines surveilling the area. Another squad of Marines patrolled along the valley at the bottom of Reno.

This hill had gone back and forth so many times it had worn areas from mortar fire. The trenches with high sandbag walls were all shot to hell. Razor wire, mines, and booby traps from us and the enemy scattered throughout the valley and hills. Nobody could keep track of it all. It was one big crap shoot.

We followed the squad of ten Marines past Forward Aid to a narrow draw on the front side of the ridge. Hard rain draining down into the valley caused the depressed path shaped like a "V" with the point at the top. It gave us a natural protected area to climb.

We had already met three of the men. Back on the line, Vegas had a pink superficial scar on his forehead from a stray bullet. Rock solid, Tank brought his over-the-top anger. Sergeant Dixon Mayo saw Orrin and just shook his head. I knew Orrin felt the pressure.

"Buck up. Be a man. You can do this," Orrin whispered to himself like one of Red's pep talks.

Dark by 1800, the snow on the ground lit the way, highlighting the sharp boulders and barren brush. The moon gleamed across the area. Could the enemy see our breath in the cold? I hoped not. We carefully stepped in each other's tracks. Not that we had a choice, the draw became narrower as we climbed. Orrin slipped on the slick incline. Behind him, Tank grabbed his arm so he wouldn't roll down the hill taking Tank with him.

Across the valley, shadows eerily moved. Was it the enemy or just the wind swirling gusts of snow? I wanted to ask if so much light was a good thing. It unnerved me as we crept up the draw of the hill to the sub-ridge where the main trench was.

All of a sudden, a flare lit up like a spotlight across the whole valley. We looked over the sandbag wall to the front of the hill from our side and saw twenty Chinese and North Koreans crawling under the coils of expanded concertina wire where the hill and valley met in the center. The Marines in our squad opened fire on the enemy from our left flank while another unit on the other flank of Reno did the same. The enemy scattered for some kind of cover, whether a boulder, bush, or crater.

The Marines in the draw ducked farther down into the two-foot-high depression. My heart pounded in my chest. An explosion in the draw above sent Marines flying in all directions. My ears rang from the shockwave.

Before we could react and take aim, someone shouted, "Vicar!"

Orrin hunched down and crawled upward. With zero cover, he heaved himself over the side of the high sandbag wall and into an exposed area near a rock formation just a bit higher than the North Koreans.

Wicked BRRAP-PAP-PAP-PAP came from the Chinese burp guns. I watched and prayed he wouldn't step on a landmine.

Vegas grabbed my arm keeping me from following. "Only one corpsman in danger at a time." I understood, but I didn't like it.

Next to a large rock with slightly more cover, Sergeant Mayo called out again. "Vicar!"

"I'm here. Where are you hurt?" Orrin asked beside him.

"My left knee," Mayo replied.

The flare dimmed. In the moonlight, Orrin looked down at the area where Mayo's knee should have been. Dark blood melted the snow. His lower left leg lay five feet away. Mayo didn't even realize it. Orrin quickly made a tourniquet against Mayo's thigh. To prevent an infection, he sprinkled sulfa powder on the open wound then pressed a thick bandage against the stub.

Still inside the draw, Vegas and Tank covered Orrin and Mayo with their gunfire. Adrenaline pumped through me, and I wasn't even out there. Orrin put his arm around Mayo to help him up and flinched as he stood.

"Vicar, stay down, damn it," Tank bellowed.

Just as the gunfight started, it stopped. Thank God! Was the enemy dead? Vegas, Tank, and I crawled over the sandbag wall into the crevice beside Orrin and Mayo. Orrin had made a makeshift litter using his and Mayo's guns stuck in his zipped coat.

Tank thrust his gun at Orrin. "We'll carry him. You cover us."

Orrin nodded. "We gotta hurry. He's already in shock."

"I ain't in shock, squid," Mayo said. "I could walk right out of here." He tried to get up.

"Sure, Sarge," Orrin said. Tank and Vegas were wide-eyed. "But I think you should make them carry you out like a king on his throne." He plunged a morphine shot into his other leg.

"Yeah, I'd like that," Mayo slurred.

When nobody else shouted for help nearby, Orrin held Tank's gun at the ready. The big Marines lifted the unconscious Mayo easily and carefully carried him down the side slope draw. We rounded the bottom of the hill from the side, Orrin at point, me in the rear. The other Marines in the squad continued to the sub-ridge to support the outpost. Somewhere, Sciulli and Red would help the remaining men.

Moonlight hit a glint of steel in an outcropping on the tandem hill along our narrow path between the two hills. Before I realized what he was doing, Orrin shot him. The enemy sniper fell off the parapet twenty feet onto the sharp rocks below. Shocked, I stared. I barely saw him.

At Forward Aid, Orrin and I placed Mayo on an actual litter. "There's a jeep ready," I said. "Help me, Vicar."

I handed Orrin his coat and carbine from the makeshift litter while Tank and Vegas put Mayo across the backseat of the jeep. Corpsman Ringer stayed to help any other wounded arriving. Vegas and Tank jogged away returning to the hill.

In a rush, Orrin slipped his coat back on with all his other layers then tripped into the passenger side of the jeep. He let out a pained grunt. I took off like a bat out of hell, which seemed appropriate. We were in hell.

"Are you hit?" I asked him.

"What?"

"There's blood on the shoulder of your coat."

"There is? It can't be mine."

"You're as white as a ghost."

"His leg laid five feet away," Orrin said. He shivered. From the cold or from what just happened? Probably both—like me.

At Able Med, corpsmen and Dr. Levitt whisked Mayo away. I dragged Orrin to the all-purpose x-ray area for privacy.

"I killed a man," Orrin said, sitting on the exam table. He stared at the eye chart across the room.

"Kill or be killed. You saved Mayo's life," I replied, stripping off Orrin's bandoliers, vest, coat, and shirt.

Orrin remained silent as I cleaned and stitched his left arm where a bullet had gone right through. Luckily, the bullet had missed the bone. Dr. James came in and approved my handiwork.

"I want you in recovery for two hours," James said. Before Orrin could protest, the doctor turned to me. "Sling him up."

After James left, I helped Orrin put on the sling. "A two-hour nap sounds good to me."

"I don't need it."

"Orders," I replied.

"Special treatment? None of the other corpsmen get to take a nap. I can handle my first patrol."

"You were shot. Rest for a bit, then take confessions, Vicar," I said.

Orrin sat on a cot and watched me make room for more wounded. I could tell he wasn't going to sleep.

"Vicar, are you hurt, too?" Dale Kaminski, the nondescript twin to his now dead friend Brian McClellan, asked a few cots down. His legs were in casts.

Orrin moved to the stool beside him. "They winged me. How are you feeling?"

"All I could think about was my parents getting THE letter."

"Well, they won't now. What's the doctor say?" Orrin asked.

"I'm going home," he said, tearing up. "But I'm leaving my buddies. Who'll have their backs?"

"I will," Orrin replied, standing. "Just think about home. Get some rest."

With a stack of charts, I nodded at Father Doggett, a petite man with delicate features standing in the doorway. He took a seat next to Orrin at the table in the corner of the room. From his chair, Orrin fidgeted. Was he feeling the pain after that adrenaline rush?

"Have you heard how Sergeant Mayo is doing?" Orrin asked quietly.

"They flew him to the hospital ship. Are you a man of the cloth?" Father Doggett asked. He must have heard Kaminski call him Vicar.

"No sir," Orrin said. "Like you, I can listen and keep a secret."

Would Orrin keep his own secret of killing a man? More lies to his parents?

Slowly rotating his wounded shoulder, Orrin scanned the full room, quiet for now. I moved from one man to the next checking their vitals. I was sure Orrin would be there for the men when they woke up. Orrin had earned a reputation for listening. It's as if the men just needed to know they weren't alone. We all seemed to feel the same, deep down—afraid of dying, afraid of living, afraid of being alone. I certainly felt that way. I knew Orrin did, too, but he wouldn't admit it. He concealed his fears from everyone, maybe even himself.

Orrin sighed and picked up the paper and pencil left on the table for Marines who wanted to write home about their sad or happy news. Would Orrin tell his parents the truth this time?

1 January 1953

Dearest Mother and Dad,

Don't mind the Red Cross stationery. I ran out of paper and this was all I could find. We went on a hike last night. In the middle of winter, the hills are barren of life and greenery so the hike was quite boring and cold.

With the moon shining at night, it was just about as good as daytime. I saw a buzzard perched on an outcropping overlooking a hill. I killed it. It seemed to search for death. I didn't want it near us.

A new year and new resolutions. Do you have any? I'm working to bulk up and maybe be a little neater. Rawley thinks I'll break that one before sundown. He may be right. I'm going to hit the sack now. I'll write more soon.

All the love a son can give,

Orrin

CHAPTER EIGHT

11 January 1953

Dearest Mother and Dad,

I received your package yesterday and I want to thank you for the batteries and peanut brittle. I miss your fried chicken. We had some in the mess tent but it was too greasy and dried out at the same time. I'm trying to eat more to build muscle. It doesn't help that the foods here are bland and aren't my favorites that you fix. Something to look forward to when I get home.

Have a good time on your trip to Memphis. Give Aunt Myrna and Uncle Ned my best. Tell Jimmy that my bowling average is getting better although I haven't bowled in a while.

It was a big surprise for me to learn that Rawley has never bowled. He even has a bowling alley just down the street from where he lives. We're going to play as soon as we can. He says he'll win with beginner's luck. I won't care one way or another. Please keep writing.

    All the love a son can give,

    Orrin

IN THE MORNING BEFORE CHOW, Dr. James and I tested Orrin's range of motion for his left shoulder in the empty operating room. Orrin hardly winced now. He had worked hard on the rehab. He could have gone back to the Reserve Hospital to do it, but he may not have been reassigned to Able Med. I was so happy he stayed. Orrin made my life in Korea bearable. James gave the official okay for full duty before leaving.

"I swear I'm ready," Orrin said.

"You don't have to prove to anyone that you know your stuff. We already know," I said.

"To prove to myself," he replied.

In the chow line, we saw a few of the disheveled George Company Marines at a table in the corner. Back from the front, Hey Baby gave us a glad-you're-still-alive nod and smile. Orrin returned it with a slight wave. One of the Marines turned to see who Hey Baby had acknowledged. We had met Corporal Anthony Sarino during the smallpox inoculations. I didn't know much about Sarino except he had a wife and daughter. Sarino waved then turned back around.

Corpsman Lukas Sciulli grabbed a tray in front of us and pointed to the biscuits and gravy and powdered eggs. Private Washing slapped them on his tray, then onto Orrin's tray, and then onto mine. No longer boisterous, Sciulli wasn't as annoying and seemed quieter after his first patrol. We understood that now. Joining Sciulli, Orrin picked at his food. Sciulli wolfed down his.

"Whoa, where's the fire?" I asked, sitting across from them.

"I don't want to be late relieving Parsons in the ward. He said he'd report me if I was late again."

Sciulli stood up, turned green, and then puked his breakfast back onto his tray. The same gray chunky gravy. In a chain reaction, the men around him dry heaved and quickly moved away. Frozen in his spot, Sciulli broke into a sweat and stared at his tray.

"Get the hell out," I yelled.

Ready to puke again, he picked up his tray and ran for the exit. It just so happened the arrogant Dr. Daniels walked in. Sciulli's tray of vomit hit him square in the chest. I laughed. I couldn't help it. The whole group tried not to throw up as they scattered out the side doors.

Outside the tent, Sciulli puked again. The smell of shit wafted toward those left inside. It wasn't the food this time. He had vomit down the front of him and diarrhea down the back. Holding a napkin over his nose and mouth, Dr. Daniels, covered in chunks of regurgitated biscuits and gravy, sent Sciulli to Battalion Med so as not to spread the stomach flu. For laughing, I had to drive him there.

By the time I returned, twenty men came down with the same thing. Without symptoms ourselves, Orrin and I put them all in two tents and opened sickbay there. We had one spare bed until I puked into a bedpan and collapsed onto it. Wearing a mask, Orrin made sure everyone had a bedpan for duel purposes. Oh, the smells! Marines turned into the biggest bunch of babies.

Corpsman Joe Garcia escorted all our wounded to Reserve. Joe needed a reprieve from the front. Before every patrol, he gorged his food and then barfed. Whatever helps us get through the tension, although it probably wasn't the healthiest way. Leaving Orrin to mother the men, the doctors left for Easy Med since all the wounded from the front would head there.

When we weren't puking or pooping, we slept in our own sweat. Quite disgusting. We complained and whined that our symptoms were worse than the others'. Orrin held his tongue and let us vent. He was a saint. I wondered if this was how Grandma felt taking care of me—unappreciated. The next day, Orrin continued to clean soiled bedpans. He said he wanted to take a boiling shower in antiseptic.

At 1200 on the third day, Orrin carried around cups of chicken broth. All our fevers had broken and most of us were starving—but not for biscuits and gravy. The cook had taken that off his menu.

Though looking pasty, Hey Baby said he felt well enough to write his letters to the gals back home. In the next cot, Anthony Sarino rolled a small stone between his fingers as he stared at the ceiling of the tent. Hey Baby had called him "Turq," but Sarino looked Pilipino to me.

Orrin set a glass of water beside him. "A good luck charm?"

Sarino snapped out of his deep thought and showed him the smooth stone. "It's from my wife. Turquoise protects against negative energy." Ah, I understood now. Turq stood for Turquoise.

Marshall laughed. "You still got the flu."

"I'm still alive," Sarino replied. Orrin nodded and turned to leave. "Uh, hey Vicar, do you have any paper? I want to write home."

"I'll find you some," Orrin replied.

Rubbing my head, I sat up on my elbow. "Don't ask Hey Baby for any. He needs it all for his many girlfriends." The lame zinger drained me as I fell onto my damp pillow and groaned.

"It's true. They love me," Hey Baby replied.

"Just pick one already," Sarino said.

"Why?" he asked.

Shaking his head, Orrin walked away. The only doctor at Able Med, Colonel Levitt, entered the tent and checked each man. Orrin followed him with a clipboard to transcribe his orders. Levitt kicked everyone out to the land of the living except me.

As Orrin gathered our soiled linens in the vacated tent, he started sweating, swore, and then grabbed the closest bedpan. Needing the tent for any wounded that came in on the next raid, Orrin and I staggered to our bunks in the corpsmen's tent, climbed in, and fell asleep.

A few hours later, Levitt entered. "Ringer and Connor are on tonight's patrol."

"Sir, Connor's sick," Ringer said.

Orrin groaned at his name and sat up.

Levitt looked at him, felt his head, and nodded. "Parsons, you're up."

Red glared at Orrin. Wincing at the skip, Orrin sacked back out. In the morning drenched in sweat, he unzipped his sleeping bag. It looked so wet he could probably ring it out. Leaving it open to dry out, he stripped out of his soaked clothes. When Sciulli left the tent, a gust of winter encouraged Orrin to hurry.

I handed Orrin a cup of chicken broth from the top of our oil stove. "Should you be up yet?"

"I'm much better now," he replied. "Where's everybody?"

I hesitated as he took a sip. The salty broth would be heaven to his wrenched stomach. It was for me when I was sick.

When I didn't answer, Orrin looked like he'd vomit again. "What's happened?"

"Well," I started, rubbing my hand through my brown curls. I needed a haircut—barely regulation. "I'll give it to you straight."

Orrin moved his wet sleeping bag aside and sat on the cot. He set his mug beside him, spilling it. Ignoring the mess, he laced up his winter boots.

"The enemy tried to take Hill 98," I said.

Orrin winced.

"Major Beck wanted to keep that hill whatever the cost. Ringer was hit in the chest and died where he dropped."

"What about Red?" he asked. His replacement.

101

"A Bouncing Betty hit him in both legs and abdomen. They flew him to the hospital ship."

"That would have been me," Orrin whispered.

"No, you're not stupid enough to stray from the foot paths," I said, trying to make him feel better. It didn't work.

"Why them and not me?" he asked.

"Someone up above has a plan for you, my friend," I replied.

Orrin rubbed his eyes and mumbled, "Will we ever leave this hell? So many won't."

16 January 1953

Dearest Mother and Dad,

Mother, my buddy Rawley says the hand of God must be on me. I had the stomach flu and a one hundred and four fever. I missed out on going for a hike. A couple corpsmen were injured. So I guess you shouldn't worry about me. Just say a few prayers for the Marines so that we'll all go home soon. Anyway, Able Med is shiny and clean. We disinfected the whole camp. Not a germ in sight now. We'll be ready for wounded—if we get any.

All the love a son can give,

Orrin

CHAPTER NINE

18 January 1953

Dearest Mother and Dad,

I'm happy you enjoyed your trip. Did Aunt Myrna make her family famous ambrosia? I can taste it just thinking about it. I can't believe Little George is ten already. I hope you gave them my best.

Able Med is back to normal after our minor flu epidemic. Before I was sick, I took care of these babies. If I haven't said it before, thank you, Mother, for taking care of me when I was younger.

The other night, the Chinese tried to pull some kind of funny trick. They went out about a hundred yards in front of our lines and set up some signs. The next morning, we found two large signs and four smaller ones. They also put out three big crates. We can't tell what's in them, and we're not checking because they have a bunker behind the *signs with a machine gun inside. Not to worry, Mother, I only saw it through the field glasses. The 11th Marines and their artillery threw a couple rockets at it.*

Well, it's getting cold, too cold for snow it seems. It's below zero so we stay inside as much as possible. We're "clutch platoon" tonight which means we just moved into Dad Company position on the MLR while their platoon moves to an outpost. I'm doing my part on phone watch in the command post bunker, the safest place to be, so I will have to close for now.

All the love a son can give,

Orrin

THE COLD WIND WHIPPED THROUGH the open door of the C.P. bunker. Whoever designed it was nuts. The front and only entrance faced the enemy. One lucky mortar round would cook us all. That's why Orrin sat with the phone in a canvas bag on his lap beside the doorway by the sandbags. I sat on the other side, waiting for orders. Our plan was to be the first ones out, which might be flawed if the enemy targeted our bunker. No winners here.

Our ice-cold sandbag dwelling barely fit nine empty bunks, three beds high for the Marines stationed here, and a tiny table and chair for Major Webster. It was smaller than the bunkers at Able Med. Webster stared at his map with the main line of resistance (MLR) marked on it— guaranteed to be the same at the end of the day, every day. We made no headway, but neither did the enemy.

Lieutenant Kingston waited for orders. Both men were fresh off the plane for their first look at combat. Orrin and I studied the map on the wall of the trench system. Almost into the valley, the listening posts were the farthest from us and the closest to the enemy. The worst places to be.

Outposts were up high along the edge of the ridges throughout the hill crests. With our communication line constantly broken, outposts would send a runner who may or may not get the messages to the intended party. A terrible job to have. The trench system along the side and front of the hill was so rocky that sandbags created higher walls for more cover.

"Lieutenant, they'll call if they need our help," Webster said.

While Orrin waited for orders to call someone or for the phone to ring, I watched a huge rat drag a half-eaten c-ration container under the back bunk. The Marines called the rats "bunker bunnies." That one was almost as big as a cat. I would not be sleeping in here. It looked strong enough to drag me under there.

Having seen it too, Orrin shuddered as the phone rang. "C.P.," he said. He paused to listen. "Major, we got fifteen Chinese crawling up our front."

Webster yanked the phone out of his hand. He pointed at Kingston to go outside and check. As soon as he stepped outside, the sound of burp guns exploded throughout our area. Shot through the head, Kingston fell backward into the bunker. Blood and brain matter covered the bunker bunny that didn't look fazed a bit.

Major Webster tossed the phone at Orrin. "Get the 11th on the line."

Orrin cranked the handle and listened. "The phone's dead."

"Damn it. Follow me. And for God's sake, stay low."

With deep breaths, we grabbed our medic bags and our carbines then followed Webster into the trench in front of the bunker. Staying low almost at a crawl, we couldn't see over the top of the trench side to the slope below without getting our heads blown off. Case in point: Kingston.

The Chinese were shooting above our heads but a well-placed grenade would do some harm. With a flare gun in one hand and pistol in his other, Webster pointed Orrin and me toward the left trench to flank the enemy while he went to the right. Okay, sure. I prayed we'd meet up with the Marines first.

Men shouted as they traded gunfire in the chaos. I had no idea where anyone was. The darkness in the middle of Korea scared the shit out of me. Fright helped me ignore the cold. With our guns ready, we crept as fast as we thought we should. It was too easy to get lost so I kept my hand on Orrin's shoulder in front of me. I'm not too proud to create a daisy chain. As we rounded a curve, the flare lit the area. We peeked over the side to see the Chinese crawling past our razor wire almost to our trench.

Before I could set my gun on the top of the sandbag wall, Marines on our left fired, dropping a few.

"Throw grenades," Sergeant Lee Everette yelled. I liked Everette. He didn't tolerate stupidity.

While Everette fired his weapon, Orrin took two grenades and threw one. It landed in a group of four. Exchanging a look, we were horrified by their screams of pain. We focused back on a North Korean climbing up the slope six feet from us.

"Here," Orrin shouted, making a hook with his finger indicating they were just below us.

We couldn't see how many because of the high trench wall, so Orrin jumped up and peeked again. He tossed the second grenade over the side. It took out three. The Marines fired on the rest.

Looking back the way we had come, I heard a man groaning. I rushed over. "Vicar!" I yelled.

With his gun and medic bag, Orrin hurried back toward me. As the flare burned out, he reached for his flashlight and flipped it on, keeping it low. On my knees, I leaned over Major Webster, who was now unconscious. Blood covered his chest.

"I can't do this myself," I said, pressing a thick bandage against Webster's chest. "His lung collapsed."

"Okay, do you have tubing? I have some cellophane to create a seal," Orrin replied, setting his gun aside.

"Yeah, can you do it while I keep pressure on this other wound?"

Holding the flashlight under his armpit, Orrin scrambled to find what he needed then he went to work. After a minute, Orrin tested the seal around the tubing to see if it would hold. It did.

Next, we needed to get Webster to Forward Aid and a chopper. The burp gun sounds faded from heavy to a couple shots, to none. Either our guys got them all or they retreated. While we made a makeshift litter, two Marines, Turq and Vegas, joined us.

"Have you seen Sergeant Everette? We lost him," Vegas said.

"Vegas, help Turq take the major to Forward Aid. Don't jar him," Orrin said. "Rawley, help me find Everette and any other wounded."

All three of us nodded as if Orrin was an officer. In the dark, Turq and Vegas carried Webster along the side trench toward the back of the hill. Orrin and I carefully retraced our steps. Not using our flashlights, we walked carefully and listened for Everette or the enemy. Thank God we didn't have to go far.

Everette had an arm around Hey Baby, who hobbled toward us. "A broken leg I think," Everette said. "Where are the rest of the men?"

On a knee, I felt that his lower leg had swollen the size of an elephant's. I left his boot on. "Two are heading back to Forward Aid with the wounded Major Webster," I said. "Kingston's dead."

"The Chinese are trying to sneak up the front and sides of the trenches," Orrin said.

"Help Marshall while we check," Everette asked. "If you see any Marines, send them this way."

We helped Hey Baby down and around the side of the hill. We filled in the Marines on what Orrin had seen as we passed them in the darkness.

"It's like we're in training at Pendleton and I'm saving you again," Orrin said.

Hey Baby snorted. "Except here my balls are gonna freeze off."

Inside the Forward Aid bunker, we heard our mortar fire on the other side of Hill 98. On bunks, four Marines had injuries. Grumbling under his breath that everything was an inconvenience, Corpsman Caleb Fitzpatrick constantly sighed as he tightened the tourniquet above the ankle of a mangled foot. The frigid night slowed the bleeding. In the corner, Hey Baby stared in horror. I monitored Major Webster as we heard the chopper land.

Orrin and I loaded Webster and the Marine with a shattered foot into the helicopter. Bloody, cold, and shaken, Orrin and I helped the rest into the jeep. Fitzpatrick would stay at Forward Aid and assist Sciulli and Garcia still in the field.

My heart pounded and my hands trembled. I was just as scared as my first time on patrol. Was Orrin? I drove the crowded jeep back to Able Med where we would prepare for the next wave of wounded.

"Now that was something to write home about," I said.

"My aunt and cousins didn't even realize we're fighting a war. They wanted to know why I wasn't at the family reunion," Orrin replied, pulling up the collar of his coat to stay warm.

"Maybe they'd make a bigger deal about the war if you'd tell them the truth."

"You really tell your sister everything?" Orrin asked.

"She'd know if I didn't."

"Is that a twin thing?"

"A bossy sister thing."

We froze our tails off during the ten-mile drive to Able Med. Warm bodies tightly packed helped slightly, but frostbite would be an issue for any man outside for too long. Luckily, the wind had died down. The adrenaline kept us going throughout the night and morning as Able Med became bombarded with the wounded of Hill 98—again.

20 January 1953

Dearest Mother and Dad,

We all had our teeth checked yesterday. I guess mine were okay because the dentist didn't say anything. The PX truck came and everyone bought cookies, fruit juice, canned meat, and crackers. I bought some toothpaste and a fruit cake. It's not like the ones you make over the holidays, but it tasted good after a long day.

Rawley's sister sent him some herbs so we're hoping he'll make chili again. It'll warm us right up. They are very close. Both parents died in a car crash when they were five. That's when they moved in with their grandmother at the boarding house. Rawley said she's been the best mama to them. He doesn't see it as a tragedy but a move to a loving home. As cynical as he seems, he has a positive attitude about family. We both do.

Dad, I hope you set Aunt Myrna straight about why we're here. Will you then explain it to me again? Take care. I'll write more later.

All the love a son can give,

Orrin

CHAPTER TEN

5 February 1953

Dearest Mother and Dad,

Well, Able Med moved back across the Imjin River. We had to pack up all the canvas tents, corrugated metal buildings, and bunkers and then set them up three miles away. The wind had swept down the Imjin from north to south along the river forming a thick ice. I've never seen that happen to a fast-flowing river before. I guess it shows you just how cold it gets here.

I wouldn't mind finding a nice river to fish. Rawley says back home he fishes for carp on the local river. His grandmother makes it tasty. I'm not sure about that though. She does use all the unused parts as fertilizer in her garden.

I'm sitting here in the corpsmen's tent. The stove isn't working so I'm writing pretty fast. The oil for the stove had some water in it and froze. Maintenance will be here soon to work on it. I'll write more later. My fingers are too cold right now.

   All the love a son can give,

   Orrin

ON MY BUNK, I HALF-DOZED and half-watched the corpsmen in the tent, too tired to contribute to the banter. Orrin tucked his letter under his pillow and sat up on his sack. Caleb Fitzpatrick, a.k.a. "Mr. Angry," broke a boot lace tying them. Neatnik, Bob Waters straightened his sack for the third time until it was perfect. Lukas Sciulli monkeyed with the stove. He had a lighter against the piping.

"Uh, Sciulli, that's not a good idea," Orrin said. "The pipe's cracked."

"I'm just melting the ice."

"But the oil is flam—"

Before Orrin could finish his warning, the outside of the pipe caught fire and the flame traveled toward the excess oil.

"Take cover!" Orrin yelled.

The two other corpsmen dove under their bunks as the stove exploded. Shrapnel ripped through the tent. I yanked my blanket over my head, not that it would protect me from metal shards, but I hoped for a shield nonetheless.

Orrin started smacking my bed with a blanket to smother the fire. I scrambled to get up. Grumbling, Caleb Fitzpatrick and Bob Waters put out the flames nearest them. Smoke filled the area.

"Anybody hurt?" Orrin asked.

"I'm fine," Fitzpatrick said.

"I'm okay," I said, searching for that knucklehead, Sciulli.

"I am, too," Waters said. Always by the book, Waters would be the first to tattle.

"Uh, guys, I could use some help," Sciulli whispered.

Sprawled out on the floor, Sciulli had a small piece of shrapnel sticking out of his sternum. I flashed back to the U.S.S. *Kearsarge* and George Fullaire. Kneeling beside him, Orrin grabbed my freshly washed shirt and packed it around the wound.

"Fitz, we need a litter," Orrin yelled. "And find Dr. James."

The M.P.s flung open the door, confused by the explosion. The smoke filtered out along with Fitzpatrick.

"I'm in so much trouble," Sciulli whispered.

"You'll be on KP for a while," Orrin replied.

Our tent, sleeping bags, and probably clothes would smell like smoke for a long time. While Sciulli went to surgery, our new C.O., Derek Doerr, demanded our presents and report. Standing in front of the desk, Orrin and I waited for Doerr to hang up his phone. Doerr wasn't a doctor; he was a paper-pushing colonel. Colonel Levitt had transferred to the Battalion Reserve hospital. The lucky duck.

The C.O. slammed his phone down and growled. "Where are your guns?"

"In the chaos, we forgot, sir," Orrin replied.

"I thought I was clear. Every Marine must carry his gun and ammo. Corpsmen carry their medical packs, too."

"Yes sir. Sorry, sir," Orrin replied.

"Out," he said. After an about-face, we headed for the door, happy not having to explain what had happened.

Back in the tent in the late afternoon, we got our guns, ammo belts, and medic bags. All the guys thought this was a dumb rule. Our hands were always full.

The stove and its pieces had been removed. Small tears in the canvas leaked in the cold air. Mumbling a whole vocabulary of swear words, I ransacked Sciulli's bunk.

"He's gonna kill us all. The knucklehead," I said, holding Sciulli's size small shirt up to my large frame. Wadding it up, I chucked it back on his cot.

"How's he doing?" Orrin asked.

"It was superficial. He'll be fine," I replied.

"That damn kid has nine lives," Fitzpatrick said, lying across his sack.

"Maybe," I said. "But we don't."

"He was just trying to help," Orrin said.

"He's a pain in the ass," Fitzpatrick added.

I nodded as a couple Marines carried in our new heater/stove. With our arms full of gear, Orrin and I left our tent and headed for the chow line. Standing in the doorway, we watched Marines and corpsmen juggling their equipment and their trays. Carbines pointed every which way.

"Oh, boy," I said. "Someone's gonna get shot in the ass."

On high alert for idiots, we found a place in the corner to eat. We downed our chow rather quickly. As the men crowded into the mess, Orrin glanced at me. I nodded, and we dashed out. Entering the recovery ward, we heard a shot ring out. Shouting followed.

"Did I predict that?" I asked. Orrin snickered.

Still angry at Sciulli, I gathered the laundry, avoiding him. We'd be sleeping in a cold, smoky tent. Two Marines and Sciulli were the only ones in the ward. The others had been shipped back to either Battalion Reserve or the hospital ship.

Orrin sat beside Hey Baby who had a bad sprained ankle, not a broken leg as we'd previously thought. He would head back to his squad tomorrow. "How's the letter writing going? Still getting a stack?"

He shook his head. "A few of the girls from home found out and they all stopped writing, except Ginger Toby. She wrote one last letter saying she deserved better."

"So you see how disrespectful that was?" Orrin asked. "Maybe you should write just to her and apologize."

"What do you mean?" he asked with a blank stare.

"Never mind."

Hey Baby turned on his side, clearly wanting to sleep. Orrin checked on the sleeping Ken Thompson who had a belly wound. He'd be shipped out on the next bus for Reserve. Luckily—or unluckily, depending on how you looked at it—the bullet missed his organs, and he would eventually go back to the MLR.

While I kept busy at the table, Orrin sat beside Sciulli. He pulled back the bandage to check the wound. Six stitches. "Painful?" Orrin asked.

"I can handle it. Dr. James said I'll have light duty for a few days."

"KP?"

"No. Since the snow melted, Doerr wants me to work in the rice paddy fields outside the fence."

Overhearing the discussion, I stopped and stared at them. Orrin cringed. "That can't be right. They're mined," Orrin said.

Sciulli swallowed. "Mined? Do you think that's my punishment?"

"He must not know," Orrin replied.

I, too, hoped that was the reason.

Colonel Derek Doerr wanted to change everything. He was strict. The fact he wouldn't listen was a sign of a bad leader. The men said he was as dumb as a door. I'd started that rumor.

6 February 1953

Dearest Mother and Dad,

Our new commanding officer is keeping us prepared so at a moment's notice we'll be ready for combat. Don't worry, Mother. It's just a precaution.

We have a new stove in our tent. The old one just fell apart on us. We had quite a mess to clean up, but we're nice and warm now.

The way the corpsmen are coming in I'll be home after just nine months here. That means only six more months to go. I'm enclosing a check for $150 for you to deposit into my savings. I'm still trying to decide what kind of car to buy.

All the love a son can give,

Orrin

CHAPTER ELEVEN

17 February 1953

Dearest Mother and Dad,

I just received your wonderful letter and package and am happy to say that I am fine. Thank you for the shaving kit and two pairs of fur-lined gloves. They are just perfect.

The sugared nuts are delicious, too. I had a few and shared the rest with the men. Boy, you really cheered them up.

Rawley's sister crocheted us thick wool hats. They sure are warm under our helmets. I'll give a set of gloves to Rawley, and we'll be ready for the rest of the winter.

I've been spending time with the Marines in our recovery ward. Brave men that I'm proud to help. They have been through the ringer with this fighting. We'll all be glad to go home hopefully soon.

Please keep writing. Mail call is the only thing I look forward to over here.

All the love a son can give,

Orrin

AT 0300, THE ABLE MED P.A. System cracked on. "Incoming. All shifts report."

Filled with dread, we jumped out of our sacks. Already dressed and in his boots, Orrin caught his foot on the sleeping bag and fell flat on the floor. Still a klutz. After wadding up his sleeping bag, he left it on the bed and grabbed his winter coat, new hat, and new gloves. Out the door before the rest, he ran up the hill to the chopper pad sliding a few times in the light snow. I passed him in the jeep. Swirling the snowflakes, the helicopter with two external litters landed.

Orrin raced to the left side, quickly checking the tag. "Chest wound," he yelled. Putting more pressure on the thick dressing soaked in blood, he flagged me over. We each grabbed an end of the litter.

After we lifted the man onto the jeep, Orrin jumped up and reapplied the pressure. I drove down to the O.R. knowing this Marine would be first. Holding on with the other hand, Orrin glanced at the Marine's face for the first time.

"Shit," Orrin said.

"What?" I said glancing back at him.

Paling, he looked at me. "It's Sciulli."

I accelerated.

"Do your job. Do your job," Orrin repeated to himself over and over. "He'll be okay. Just get him to surgery."

We set the litter on the first table. Dr. "Arrogant" Daniels felt for a pulse. "He's dead."

Orrin just stared at the doctor as if he didn't understand what he'd said. Daniels said it so casually, like he didn't know who Sciulli was. Biting my tongue, I pushed Orrin in motion. We carried the litter and Sciulli back out.

After covering him with a sheet, Orrin took a deep breath. "Buck up," he whispered.

Clenching my jaw, I mumbled, "Damn knucklehead couldn't stay out of harm's way. Just when I started to tolerate him, he dies on us." I let my anger take over my sadness.

We brought the men into the O.R. then left with either a recovering Marine or more dead. Numbing our emotions, we forced ourselves to focus on the living.

After twenty-four hours, the injured men rested in the recovery wards. One hundred and twenty Marines injured. Eighteen dead. All for one lousy hill.

Jumping into my sack, I closed my eyes. I wanted to forget this day, this year, this war.

In the morning, Orrin shook me awake. "We've got twenty minutes to report to B Ward."

Still tired like the whole camp, we went to the mess for coffee. Asleep or awake, we were in a nightmare. In the recovery ward, we looked at the lines of Marines.

Some slept peacefully knowing they were alive and away from the MLR. Others tossed and turned believing they were still there.

While I started on our paperwork, Orrin sat beside an agitated man with his shoulder and arm in a sling and bandages on his abdomen.

"Hey," Orrin whispered. "You'll be all right. Be calm, so as not to tear your stitches."

He opened his eyes. "I don't want to go back to that hell."

"I know," Orrin said. He couldn't confirm where he'd be going next. "Have you written home lately? I could help you if you'd like."

"Maybe later."

"Sure. Do you have plans after the war?"

He smiled. "I'm going to marry my sweetheart and work with my dad selling cars."

Orrin perked up. "Really? I'm saving up for a car. I'll pick your brain for the best one later."

With a nod, he relaxed, and Orrin moved on to the next agitated Marine, Sydney Camp.

"I heard a few of the guys call you Vicar. You a real one?" Camp asked.

"No." Orrin chuckled. "Just a nickname."

"The holder of secrets," Corpsman Caleb Fitzpatrick said behind them.

Orrin shrugged. "Sydney, what are your plans after the war?"

"I don't know," Camp replied. "I haven't thought much about it. What are yours?"

"My dad's a doctor at our local VA hospital. I'll probably follow in his footsteps."

"My dad's an ironworker who builds skyscrapers in Chicago. I'm afraid of heights and will not be following in his."

"Yikes," Orrin said with a laugh. "What do you like to do?"

"Read."

"Do you have a book in you that needs to be written?" he asked.

Camp paused. "Oh, I just might." The mental wheels seemed to be turning as Camp stared off into the distance.

With a smile, Orrin moved to the next Marine. He enjoyed listening to the men's plans. The conversations took them home to a better place.

For me, I wanted to buy a house with a large, fenced yard and raise Alaskan Malamutes. That loyal breed is beautiful. I liked dogs more than most people.

20 February 1953

Dearest Mother and Dad,

I think I have a line on the kind of car I want. I got some great advice about the different makes and models.

Rawley has an old Ford truck that he keeps running. Since I'm not mechanically inclined, I'll let the professionals tinker with my car.

I heard one of the boys sing a song the other day and I think it is really good. It's called "The Soldier's Last Letter".

It's quite a sad song when sung at the right time and makes one sit down and think about his mother and what she means to him. I guess it hit me a bit hard the first time I heard it.

This letter won't be very long tonight. I just wanted you to know I am thinking of you and I miss you.

All the love a son can give,

Orrin

CHAPTER TWELVE

19 March 1953

Dearest Mother and Dad,

I expected to get a letter from you tonight but nothing came so I decided to sit down and write you one. I hope to hear from you tomorrow. The mail at night is about the only thing that we have to look forward to.

I got a letter from Aunt Myrna. It sounds like Uncle Ned isn't doing well. She thinks it's lung cancer? What does the doctor say? She asked me how my vacation was going. I don't think she understood where I am. Maybe it's better that way, especially if Uncle Ned is ill.

We're leaving for a hike soon to stay in shape so I better hit the sack while I can.

All the love a son can give,

Orrin

IT FIGURED THE MOTOR POOL gave us another jeep without a cover, saving the good ones for the officers. It started raining the moment Orrin and I left Able Med. At dusk and in a hurry, we continued toward Forward Aid. The heavy rain soaked through our raingear, leaving us cold, wet, and irritable.

I wanted behind the wheel in the rain because Orrin drove too fast in general, although I flew down the muddy road anyway. Silent, Orrin flinched at the stinging rain pelting his face. It soured his mood even more.

"What's eating you?" I asked. "You've been mad since mail call."

"People back home don't even know where Korea is or that we're fighting in a war."

I nodded. "Too busy idolizing Marilyn Monroe and James Dean. Hollywood has Technicolor now."

"Men have died. For what? These damn hills have gone back and forth since we've been here. It makes me so angry."

"Why don't you tell them that?" I asked. It was rhetorical. I already knew why, but I liked pushing him. He usually pushed back, as best friends do. Orrin had said he gained comfort in downplaying his experiences while I felt a healing purge.

Squinting at the non-existent road, Orrin wiped the rain from his face and remained silent. I leaned forward against the steering wheel, then suddenly cranked it, swerving to the right. We bounced over a few leafless bushes. The rain and mud washed out the road. It looked like a stream had always been there. I drove up and over an area that hadn't made a gorge of the dirt yet.

"We better tell the bus driver about that," I said.

Orrin nodded and held on. Between the heavy rain and the dimming day, I didn't think we had to worry much about snipers. We arrived at Forward Aid expecting a frenzy. Instead, two corpsmen, rule master Bob Waters and grumpy Caleb Fitzpatrick, smoked cigarettes in the doorway of the bunker that butted up against the large hill.

Orrin and I jumped out of the soaked jeep and headed for cover. Inside the bunker, we shook out our raingear, remaining wet underneath.

"Why didn't you have the top up?" Waters asked.

"We wanted fresh air," I replied. Waters nodded as if he wanted a casual Sunday drive through Korea, too.

Before I lost my temper, Orrin said, "We raced up here. The call said we had wounded."

"The Marines are heading up to Bunker Hill later tonight. Maybe Sergeant Everette wanted extra hands,"

Fitzpatrick said. "You know the military. Hurry up and wait."

While I called to warn the bus driver about the river crossing the road, Orrin lay down on an empty bunk. Maybe we could snooze before the action started. I didn't bother changing, especially if we had to go get wounded in action (WIA). Listening to the rain, I thought about the sound at night back home—background music to help me fall asleep.

"I hope I'll still love the rain when I get home," I said.

"Me, too," Orrin replied with a sigh.

Mortar fire boomed like thunder and had the corpsmen abruptly awake and alert. The North Koreans hit the hill on all sides. Blasts came close to our bunker. With loaded guns at the ready, the four men waited. None of us looked comfortable holding our medical bags, our weapons, and the rest of our gear.

At the back of the bunker, I yelled, "What the hell?"

The rainwater flowed down the hill and washed away the dirt from under the timbers and sandbags of the bunker weakening the structure. Most bunkers on the reverse slopes were heavily built. The surplus of sandbags on the roofs protected the wounded under artillery fire. Would a direct hit bring down the bunker tonight? Another close mortar shook our shelter making the wood frame creak as it shifted.

"Everybody out!" Waters yelled.

"And get hit by mortar fire?" Fitzpatrick asked.

"Stay by the entrance," Waters said.

Loaded down with all the medical supplies, our guns, and our ammo, we crowded around the entrance ready to hop out if necessary. Waters picked up the phone to call for an update.

"The line's dead. Where's the radio?" Waters asked.

Orrin handed it to him and we waited. At 0130, the radio squawked. Men were wounded.

"Connor, Armstrong, drive the jeep as far as you can toward the fighting. We'll figure out some kind of cover in this downpour," Waters said.

Under heavy fire and rain, we drove to the side. We stopped before the draw with sandbag walls, another river down its middle. With our medic bags, carbines and a rolled-up litter, we slowly climbed and cautiously looked for the nearest Marine. Orrin slipped and smashed his knee on the rock. He winced but remained silent. Not that being quiet mattered in the downpour with artillery racket. I could shout and I couldn't hear me. At the top, we crept down the main trench. Well, Orrin limped. I talked to a

Marine who was shooting over the sandbag wall. Orrin squatted and waited.

I turned to him and swore. "Listening post," I said, pointing to the battlefield at the farthest sub-trench, the outpost closest to the enemy.

Orrin nodded, and we focused on the wounded Marine who needed our help. With the rolled-up litter under our arms, we held our guns ready and worked down the trench toward the valley between our hill and the enemy's. Along the route, we passed Marines who fired toward the center zone. At the end of the snakelike sub-trench, the listening post had two wounded.

"Thank God! I wasn't sure the call got out before our line was cut. I've been trying to protect our flank, but—" Vegas was rambling from the stress.

"Where are you hurt?" Orrin asked. Flashes of light from the mortar fire gave us brief sight to our surroundings.

"My left calf and my hand. I'll be okay now. Help Biggie. He was hit in the gut."

We set the litter down to check the men. Orrin quickly bandaged Vegas's leg and then hand. A bullet had gone right through his palm. I went to work on Biggie, who was a racist and hated everyone. He enjoyed killing the North

Koreans. Orrin and I thought he was a sociopath and had stayed away from him.

"We were supposed to get support. We haven't yet," Vegas mumbled.

Along with the hammering rain, bullets hit the dirt and sandbags around us. A mortar exploded twenty feet away, causing dirt to rain down. The trench protected us somewhat.

"Vegas, hand Rawley what he needs from my bag while I watch for the enemy," Orrin said, picking up his carbine.

George Biggs took another shot to the chest. Semi-conscious, he stared at me. "Damn gook killed me," he mumbled, as if shocked by the fact.

Orrin kept his eyes on the valley, guarding us from the North Koreans and Chinese.

"We need to get Vegas out of here," I said.

"Go. I'll cover you," Orrin said.

The 11th Marines' mortar fire had kept the enemy away from our flank, a little too close for comfort in this rain, though. I put my arm around Vegas and we plodded up the trench line toward the main one. I dragged the litter behind us. Every muscle in my legs and back ached. I embraced the pain. Free of pain meant I was dead.

Leaving Biggie's body at the listening post for now, Orrin propped his carbine on the top of the trench's sandbag until Vegas and I got to the first bend. I yelled at Orin, but the rain and artillery made my ears ring. I didn't think he heard me. Finally, Orrin moved toward us, his head above the wall.

"Get your damn head down!" I screamed.

While scanning the area in the valley that lit up like flashes of lightning, Orrin stared at a brief blaze higher up the enemy's hill. A large gun shot across the valley and hit a section of our hill's main trench. Then the gun rolled back into the cave for cover.

"Orrin, I need some help!" I struggled to lay the unconscious Vegas on the litter.

Orrin took the end of the litter, and we worked up to the main trench. A blast exploded the listening post where we had just been. I felt the percussion in my chest. We almost dropped Vegas.

We followed the draw down the side to the jeep. Water flowed and Orrin mumbled a prayer not to slip again. As we set Vegas across the front of the jeep, Fitzpatrick parked his jeep beside us.

"Rawley, take him to Forward. I'll stay," Orrin said.

"No," I said. "Fitz, take Vegas. I'm going back with the Vicar."

Fitz switched jeeps and happily left the MLR. Sloshing through the water, we slowly huffed back up the draw and then moved, swiftly yet cautiously, toward the noise along the main trench. Orrin rushed ahead of me.

"Vicar, thank God," Alexander "Hey Baby" Marshall said, holding his arm across his body protecting it. He was sitting in the flooding trench. "I can't feel my arm."

A severed nerve? Orrin added a bandage to the wound. Then we wrapped his arm, securing it against his body.

"Can you walk?" Orrin asked him. He nodded. "Go toward Forward Aid. Try not to jar your body."

"The draw is a fast-moving river. Be careful," I added.

Hey Baby disappeared into the darkness while we continued the other way toward the destroyed command bunker. We sent the wounded men who could walk to Forward Aid. The rest of the Marines kept watch on the downward slope. At the crumbled bunker, we found Tank trying to move sandbags.

"Who's inside?" Orrin asked.

"Major Ainsworth and Sergeant Turner."

"We'll move the sandbags. You focus on the enemy," Orrin said.

Tank nodded. "I can do that."

We moved the heavy soaked sandbags. "This can be your new workout to build some bulk," I said.

"Sergeant Mayo would be happy to hear it," Orrin replied.

Ainsworth called out from inside.

"Just a couple more bags to move! Anyone hurt?" Orrin asked.

Through a narrow hole, Major Ainsworth said, "We're okay. What's going on out there? Our lines were cut."

"Tank!" Orrin shouted. "Tell the Major what's going on." We hadn't a clue.

Orrin took watch over the tall wall of the trench as the trade of gunfire continued. With Ainsworth and Turner freed, Orrin told them about the Chinese cave, its big gun, and where to find it.

"It's camouflaged from here. From below, it looked as big as our M2," Orrin said. "Tucked right inside a cave."

"It would have to be a tunnel to have a huge gun hidden inside the slope," Sergeant Turner said.

Ainsworth nodded. "Sergeant, get me a working radio. Let's call in an artillery strike."

Orrin saw a gash on the side of the major's head. "Sir, you're bleeding."

"Minor. Take the trench farther down for any wounded."

"Yes sir," I replied.

Crouching, we moved down the dark trench lit only by the explosions in the valley and a flare in the sky. The sound of carbines getting louder helped us identify where the Marines were.

Next to Anthony "Turq" Sarino, Orrin stopped. "Anyone yelling for a corpsman?"

"Yeah, down the hill on the other side of the barbed wire," Turq replied.

Orrin glanced over the trench wall. "What's the fastest way to get there?"

Turq made a hand motion to go up and over the side. Orrin peeked once more. With his carbine and medical bag across his shoulder, he waited. The flare dissolved. Before I could suggest an alternative, Orrin heaved himself up and over the side then slid five feet down the wet rocky hill. My chest hurt as I watched him.

"He just rushes in without a thought," I said.

"Or he does it so you don't," Turq replied.

Did he? Before I could think it through, the next flare high over the valley started the gun fire again. All I could do was ready my weapon.

Tank joined them. "What's going on?"

"The Vicar's at work," Turq said, pointing to the valley.

Orrin crawled slowly over the sharp-edged rocks, staying as low as possible.

"Corpsman!" the Marine shouted, panic in his voice.

"I'm here," Orrin said, over the shooting. "Be still. I'm almost to you."

Catching his bag on the concertina wire, he swore. Orrin should have known from past experience that it would. He reached back and unhooked it. I blew out a breath. Orrin crawled toward the Marine ten yards away almost in the center of the fighting. When the flare burned out, Orrin moved quicker and made it to the Marine as the next flare rose. The rain put them out faster than normal. The Chinese burp guns and our carbines sounded loud even in the downpour. I strained to hear the men speaking.

"What's your name, Marine?" Orrin asked.

"Johnny Johnson," he replied. On his back, he kept his eyes tightly closed as the rain pelted his face. His helmet nowhere in sight.

"I'm Connor. Where are you hit?" Orrin asked, lying on his side next to him.

"Got hit in the back. I'm not in pain. I just can't move my legs."

"Can you move your arms?" Orrin asked.

"My left one."

No pain was a bad sign. Orrin reached his hand under Johnson. I watched and read Orrin's mind. A bullet may have hit his spine. Dragging him out was not an option.

Orrin wouldn't want to move him, but he needed to pack off the bleeding.

Orrin secured Johnson's neck and then tied a belt around his ankles keeping his legs straight and supported. Keeping Johnson's back aligned, Orrin turned his body to the side. I nodded that he had the right idea. He bandaged the wound then carefully turned him onto his back.

"Well, I'm gonna need help moving you, so for now, we wait." Picking up his gun, Orrin looked around the dark, rainy area.

"We?"

"I won't leave you here," Orrin said, lying on his abdomen beside him.

Johnson's face seemed to relax a little as they lay on the ground surrounded by razor wire. Listening to the gunfire, we searched for movement, our guns at the ready.

"Are you still here?" Johnson said.

"I am," Orrin replied.

"I'm afraid."

"Me, too. Once the fight is over, I'll get some help."

"What if the Chinese take this valley and hill?"

"Are you saying that I—a squid—have more faith in the Marines than a Marine?" Orrin asked. Despite our hellish surroundings and the chaos transpiring, I smiled as he lightened the mood with Johnson.

The sounds of burp guns came closer, then stopped. I froze in the main trench, watching as three Chinese quietly crept along the barbed wire, most likely looking for a break in it. Orrin slowly raised his gun. If he shot one, would he get the other two before they turned on them? I took aim from my vantage point.

Beside me, Turq sighted his weapon, too. "Don't shoot, Vicar. Let them go by," he mumbled. I also said Turq's prayer for Orrin not to shoot.

Johnson reached out with his left hand and set it on Orrin's arm, a wordless warning not to fire. Orrin, it appeared, decided not to shoot, and I was grateful for it. We all held our breath as the Chinese passed by them.

"Take cover!" Turq shouted from the main trench next to me.

Orrin shielded Johnson's body. Ten yards away, Turq's grenade exploded, killing the three enemy soldiers. A second later, half the hill, where Orrin and I saw the tunnel and huge gun, blew up. Ammo in the tunnel exploded less than a second after that. It sent a blaze straight up like a volcano, destroying the crest. The shockwave knocked us on our asses.

Then, the screams. Orrin stared and then puked. Did he think he killed all those men? As the gunfire exchange slowed, Orrin, on his hands and knees, retched more.

"God damn it, Vicar. Don't move!" I yelled.

"Are you okay?" Johnson asked.

"Yeah," Orrin replied.

The brightly burning fire helped the Marines find the rest of the interlopers who were stunned by the massive explosion. At 0200, the gunfire ceased. The skirmish was over. The Marines defended Bunker Hill, this time.

Orrin checked Johnson with his flashlight. Blood had soaked the sides of the thick bandage. "Litter!" he yelled.

In the downpour, rays of flashlights from the main trench above worked down toward them. Tank, Turq, and I slid the litter next to them under the razor wire. I crawled beside Johnson. Still alert, we stayed low in case any snipers saw us in the rain. Probably not, but no need to dance around.

"Possible spine injury," Orrin said.

With a nod, I gently helped Orrin place Johnson on the litter without twisting his spine. We carefully maneuvered the litter out, and Tank and Turq took over for us.

"I'll stay and look for WIA and KIA," Orrin said.

"We'll take him to Forward, and we won't jar him," Tank said.

"I'll stay then," I said.

Next to the razor wire broken from the grenade, we found the body parts of the Chinese men.

"I killed them all," Orrin said, glancing at the burning hill across from theirs.

"You saved the lives of many Marines," I replied.

"It makes me sick," he said, wiping what may or may not have been rain from his face.

Seven Marines had lost their lives in that fight. Exhausted at 0400, Orrin and I followed the bus of the dead back to Able Med. Our jeep seats were soaked, but at least it stopped raining. Orrin remained silent. What was he thinking?

This night would stay with us for a long time—maybe forever. It all happened within minutes. For some, it would last a lifetime.

"You saved Johnson," I said, trying to make both of us feel better.

"He's paralyzed."

"We don't know that yet."

A flare went up and lit the area. We winced. Then, two rounds of white phosphorous fired in our direction. An explosion of white engulfed the bus. As the driver staggered down the steps covered in flames, an enemy sniper shot him, mercifully. The second round landed with a thud on the road directly in front of us. Eight feet away!

Adrenaline pumping, I swerved to miss the dud taking the jeep down a ditch. Flooring it, I zigzagged, perpendicular to the road away from any other sniper attack. Orrin held on.

"God still has a plan for you, my friend," I said, silently praying I wasn't driving through a minefield.

"For you, too," Orrin replied.

Ten minutes later, I stopped the jeep. We slowly blew out breaths, looked at each other, then laughed. We lived. We had dodged a bullet—literally.

"Luck or skill?" I asked, driving toward a tree line.

"Yes," Orrin replied, bouncing across the rocky field in the darkness. "We gotta get to Able Med and report the bus, the sniper, and that dud."

The headlights dimmed the farther from the front we went. This jeep was a piece of trash.

"I think there's a road up there," Orrin said, pointing to the opening between trees.

I accelerated. Just before we reached the trees, the jeep dropped into a five-foot-deep pit. We flew over the windshield and landed in the thick mud.

"Rawley! You all right?"

"No. I'm not!"

Orrin fumbled for the flashlight in his pocket. "Where are you hurt?"

"We're standing in a mass grave," I replied.

Orrin turned on his light. Rotten mangled bodies lined the pit. Men. Women. Children. I lost count of the decomposed bodies in the eight-by-eight-foot depression. The heavy rain washed the top soil away, leaving more than twenty bodies uncovered. Many had their arms tied behind their backs, bullets through all the skulls. We scrambled to get out of the pit. He lost his boot from the suction in the mud.

I stood beside him at the top, and we watched the front of the jeep sink into the sludge. Covered in mud, we retrieved our medical bags and carbines and then walked the four miles to Able Med.

"A year ago?" Orrin asked quietly. He limped slightly wearing one filthy boot and one soaked sock.

"My guess, too," I said.

"The North Koreans did that?"

"No. If the ROK couldn't separate the guerrillas from the peasants in South Korea, that's what happened. Everyone dies."

"Why are we even here? I thought our side was better," Orrin replied.

Apparently not.

21 March 1953

Dearest Mother and Dad,

Just a few words today. Our hike was a long muddy one. They take care of the corpsmen here the best they can. We depend on the Marines and they depend on us all the way. I like how we all work together.

I would do just about anything for my buddy, Rawley. He wants to raise Alaskan Malamutes. I plan on getting his first pup from the first litter. He says they're loyal like I am. He's buttering me up. I'm betting he'll make me pay top dollar. I'll write more later.

All the love a son can give,

Orrin

CHAPTER THIRTEEN

23 March 1953

Dearest Mother and Dad,

I'm very sorry to hear your trip to New York City was called off. I know you wanted to see the sights. Maybe it's better to wait for nicer weather. Ice storms near the Atlantic sound very cold.

Rawley says the west side of Michigan has lake effect snow. He remembers six feet of snow when he was eight. Can you imagine? He and his sister made igloos. They had to get around on skis and snowshoes.

Well, yesterday a tank found a white phosphorous dud in the middle of the road. Its gunner shot it from a distance making it explode. What a sight. A few of the tanks are heading up to the MLR. The 11th Marines sure made noise the other night. It's nice for the men to have some big support.

Thank you for the banana bread and walnut fudge.
They were a hit with the guys in recovery. I tease them
that they got wounded on purpose just so they could have
your sweets.
    All the love a son can give,
    Orrin

IN ONE OF THE RECOVERY wards, Orrin and I adjusted the curtain between a Marine and one of the two Korean women in the beds. Captain Ben Sinclair, a surgeon with a specialty in plastic surgery, had operated on the women who had burns on their faces, necks, and hands.

Americans had bombed an area with napalm a year ago. The pain they must have felt. Our hearts went out to these people caught in the middle of this political war. It made us tired, physically, mentally, and emotionally. Orrin once told me his dad had served as an Army doctor in the Pacific during WWII. I wondered if he felt mentally frustrated with the politics. Orrin would never ask his dad about his experiences, because what if they both felt the same way? Orrin would have to start telling the truth, right?

Orrin and I only had three Marines and the two women in the ward. The more serious were in a different recovery room. These guys would go back on the line at some point. The woman's ten-year-old son, Kim, had been the camp's interpreter. He was also the boy who'd gone sledding down the hill with Sciulli.

Orrin talked to Kim, who helped him tend to the women, while I changed the sheets on the empty beds. I didn't mind. It reminded me of home living with Grandma at the boarding house. Changing the linens was one of my favorite jobs. Crisp, clean sheets for our visitors. Orrin was much better with people than I was.

"If they are in pain, you find me. Okay?" Orrin said to Kim.

"A-Okay, doc," the boy replied.

Tank slept. He had been grazed across the forehead with a bullet. So lucky! Who lives and who dies? How does God make that decision? The doctors wanted Tank monitored for forty-eight hours. Orrin sat next to Turq, who was trying to open his letter with one hand. He had dislocated his shoulder and now wore a sling.

Orrin took the envelope out of his hand and opened it. "Feels like pictures inside." He handed him the folded papers.

"Isabella, my daughter, is three," Turq replied, holding up the snapshot of his daughter and wife.

"A beautiful family," Orrin said, before leaving to give him privacy.

Assisting the doctor, Orrin and I helped change the bandages on the women. We made sure to give encouraging nods at their healing progress. After gathering the soiled bandages, we hadn't much else to do. I looked for busy work and spotted Turq wiping his eyes then tightening his fists. I pointed Orrin in his direction.

Orrin nodded and then sat on the stool beside him. "Do you want to talk about it?"

"My wife got a nursing job in Lubbock, Texas, so she packed up our daughter and moved there from Corpus Christi."

"She drove all that way?" Orrin asked.

He nodded. "They've been living in a motel. Well, on the first day, the doctor said his patients wouldn't like a Mexican nurse. He came right out and said it."

"That's horrible."

Turq nodded. "She's half-Mexican and she's a damn fine nurse. She's been all over the town looking for work. My pay only covers so much."

"I'm sorry."

"She's distraught and I don't know how to help her from here." He stared at their picture.

"Does she have to stay in Lubbock?" Orrin asked. What was he up to? Curious, I moved closer.

"She won't go back to Corpus Christi. I'm her only family."

"Well," said Orrin, "my dad's a doctor and my mother's a nurse at the VA hospital in Amarillo a couple hours north of Lubbock. I bet she could get a job there. They're always short-staffed."

He sat up. "Do you really think so?"

"I do. Write her a letter. I'll give you my dad's work phone number for her to set up an interview. And I'll write him to expect her call. Her name's Eloisa, right?"

Turq nodded. "Thank you, Vicar."

"You're welcome. We have to look out for each other."

I always thought Orrin was a good guy. This gesture went above and beyond. I was proud to be his best friend.

At 1400, four tanks rolled past Able Med heading for the MLR. Although the tanks would support the troops, it also meant that Able would be busy soon. It was still raining like the days before. The mud weakened the roads and bunkers. I had heard Marines spent the day rebuilding all the Forward Aid stations.

Orrin and I helped the Marines to the bus. They'd go back to the Reserve hospital. Once okayed by the doctor there, they'd be shipped back to the line.

With his good hand, Turq shook Orrin's. "Thanks again, Vicar. You've given me solace."

Orrin smiled. "Take care. See you after the war."

With all the Marines gone from his ward, Orrin replaced the soiled linens with clean ones and checked on the women. Kim sat dutifully at their side. I left for the mess tent and returned with the women's and Kim's dinner trays.

The P.A. System cracked on. Orrin and I winced at the next words. "Incoming wounded. All shifts report."

Captain Sinclair, the big burly doctor, shouted from the doorway. "Connor, Armstrong, scrub up."

"Yes sir," we replied.

The worst of the wounded were carried in first. A Marine had been shot in the chest and abdomen. Orrin and I stopped looking at their faces. Most were barely out of high school. The ones who died haunted me at night. I suspected they'd be there the rest of my life.

On autopilot, we handed Sinclair the instruments he needed. Two hours later, we replaced our gloves for the next Marine whose left leg remained in a tourniquet. Shell fragments shredded his knee and calf. We had to amputate. At the beginning of the day, the young kid could walk. Now his life was changed forever. Everyone's life had changed here. I understood why Orrin wanted to shield his parents from this horror.

We had thirty Marines crammed into just one ward. Fifty-eight total wounded, five died in surgery, and seventeen killed in action. Exhausted, Orrin and I sat at the table in the ward and drank lukewarm coffee. Glancing at the clock, I realized we had been awake for fifty-two hours. I couldn't remember the last time we ate. I wanted sleep more and hoped these Marines could relax at least for a few hours.

Most would go home, the rest shipped back to Reserve, then to the front. The cycle continued. I couldn't fault Orrin, who gave these guys happy memories in this hell of a war. But why couldn't he see that talking about this shit helped, too?

26 March 1953

Dearest Mother and Dad,

I'm sitting at the table in the recovery ward and hope you will excuse this writing. I'm very tired. We had a lot of wounded come through the last few days, but they are resting now.

I wish you'd do me a big favor. There is a Marine here whose wife is a nurse and desperately looking for work.

Eloisa and Anthony Sarino have a three-year-old daughter, Isabella. Dad, I gave them your work number. Would you see if there is a position open for her? I think Anthony would find comfort knowing she has met some nice people. I've learned from you that military families look out for each other.

Well, Garcia came to relieve us so I am going to hit the sack. I will write again soon.

All the love a son can give,

Orrin

CHAPTER FOURTEEN

13 April 1953

Dearest Mother and Dad,

I can't tell from one minute to another just what I'll be doing here. Me and a few other corpsmen from Able Med are participating in Operation Little Switch, a POW exchange.

We're optimistic that with this exchange of prisoners it will send China an offer to resume truce talks in Panmunjom. One hundred Marines from the 1st Engineer Battalion are building "Freedom Village" at Munsan-ni.

The exchange will begin April 20th, but we're having a dress rehearsal now. General Mark W. Clark and a bunch of other generals are expected to be there.

Since Able Med is located ten miles behind the lines and thirty-five miles directly north of Seoul, we'll be just one mile from "Freedom Village". Can we hope this war will be over soon? Please pray it will be so.

All the love a son can give,

Orrin

BOUNCING IN THE BACK OF the truck at 0400, Caleb "Having a Fit" Fitzpatrick, the strict rule-follower Bob Waters, Orrin, and I saw the wooden archway erected for "Freedom Village", a tent city in the middle of a flat open field. The encampment had dirt roads, a helicopter landing area, and many tents for emergency medical treatment, administration areas, and the press corps.

Along with corpsmen from Battalion Reserve, the four corpsmen from Able Med already knew our assignments. We would greet the Americans, all one-hundred-and-forty-nine of them, and escort them through the process.

Over six-hundred-and-eighty sick and wounded men from eleven nations would be exchanged, more than half of them South Koreans. In return, we were releasing six thousand, six hundred seventy North Koreans and Chinese. We heard that the imbalance of POWs was to get rid of the communist prisoners who were wreaking havoc on the prison compounds.

At 1100, the first POW truck stopped in front of the medical tent where the corpsmen stood waiting. Excitement filled the cold air. Murmurs remained respectful. We were getting our brothers back. What shape they'd be in was anyone's guess. I couldn't imagine the level of stress and anxiety they'd have.

Orrin and I were first in the line of corpsmen waiting to help. A corpsman in the truck motioned for us to approach. We hurried up the wooden steps at the back and carried the Marine on a litter. The other corpsmen in line stepped forward for the next man. Some were weak and on stretchers. Most could walk. All had relieved smiles.

The reporters and cameramen honed in on Major General Edwin A. Pollack, the division commander, as he greeted Private Alberto Pizzaro-Baez of H Company, 3rd Battalion, 7th Marines.

Pollack shook his hand. "Welcome back, Private."

"Thank you, sir. Glad to be back."

Orrin and I carried the Marine into the tent. Many stations and more corpsmen waited for the men.

"Hot soup is ready when you are," I said.

"Okay."

At the first table, administration took his name, rank, and injuries for the record.

"I, uh, was wounded in the leg and captured at Outpost Frisco on October '52." Lifting the blanket from his litter, he showed them his leg. "Gangrene set in. They amputated."

"We'll get you new bandages and have our doctor look you over," the lieutenant said.

The Marine nodded and lay back on the litter. Exhaustion had set in; he remained silent. Orrin handed him a mug of broth while the doctor gave him a checkup.

Afterward, we escorted him in a wheelchair to the mess tent for a sturdier meal. Reporters surrounded him.

"How'd they treat you?" one reporter asked.

"It got better toward the end," he replied. "Can I call my mom?"

The press corps found a phone and filmed the call. He would have no privacy for a while.

"Mom, it's Al. I'm safe now."

We heard his mother sobbing through the phone.

"I'll see you soon," he said.

Once the private was settled, Orrin and I went back to the corpsmen line to help the next POW returning from his ordeal. One Marine they escorted had lost two toes to frostbite. All the men were dehydrated and weak from malnutrition. We helped many during the week.

The last man we carried was a fellow corpsman. While waiting for the doctor to give him his checkup, he started crying.

"I tried to take care of the wounded, but I didn't have any medical supplies. I wasn't good enough," he whispered. His body shook at what he thought was a failure to fulfill a great responsibility.

Orrin took his hand. "My dad was a POW in Japan during WWII. As a doctor, he tried his best to help the men in his charge, too. You made do with what you had. These men are still alive, and it's probably thanks to you." While the corpsman sobbed, Orrin sat beside him, a hand on his shoulder offering silent support. I was constantly amazed at how he always said the right thing.

The week flew by as we helped the American POWs readapt. When asked about their treatment, more than half of the men kept mum. The internal scars of war would outweigh the physical ones. Worn out, we climbed into the truck and headed back to Able Med.

As we pulled into the compound, the dreaded P.A. System announced, "Incoming in thirty minutes."

"I thought the truce talks would stop the fighting for a while," I grumbled, sliding out of the truck. Apparently, it was only talk.

Our C.O. sent Orrin and Fitzpatrick to the Forward Aid Station while Waters and I joined the doctors in surgery.

"Shouldn't we help prioritize the wounded in the compound first?" Waters asked, standing behind Drs. "Big Bear" Sinclair and "Arrogant" Daniels scrubbing at the sinks.

"No," Daniels said. "We have a few corpsmen from the hospital ship visiting. They may as well get their hands dirty and help."

"Are you taking out your frustrations with our rotation on the ship's corpsmen instead of their doctors?" Sinclair asked.

Waters and I shared a look. Neither of us wanted to be privy to this discussion. We all knew Daniels wanted a transfer to the cleaner ship environment, not our bloody camp.

"Hell yes," Daniels replied. "I'm going to enjoy it, too. I want to know why there isn't an exchange with those doctors."

"Because you're needed here," Doerr said from the doorway.

Daniels sneered and dried his hands. He stormed into the operating room as two Able Med corpsmen carried in the first wounded Marine. I was lucky enough to assist Dr. Sinclair while Carl Anderson, the chubby ship corpsman, observed Dr. Daniels. It wasn't long before Daniels demanded Anderson to step closer and hold the rib spreaders. Anderson turned green at the mangled chest. He started to sweat. Daniels snorted. I would bet one hundred dollars that he was smiling behind his mask.

I had a hard enough time seeing this gore and I was supposed to be used to it. I gave Anderson credit for not turning tail to vomit. It probably pissed Daniels off that he didn't.

Throughout the surgeries, I recognized a few of Orrin's techniques with bandaging. I smiled with relief that he was still okay. One hundred wounded Marines had come through Able Med in what seemed like an unending rotation. At 0600, I joined the four ship's corpsmen at their table in the mess tent. They downed their coffee black, not caring how bitter.

"Are you numb to that?" Carl Anderson asked.

"Yes and no," I replied. "I've stopped looking at their faces months ago."

"It was all so crude," Ben Colby, the lanky corpsman, said.

"Yeah, you guys see them after we clean them up with our patchwork," I said.

"How do you get those images out of your head?" Anderson said.

"I haven't figured it out yet," I replied.

They nodded sadly. "So, which one of you is the Vicar?" Colby asked.

I smiled. "Orrin Connor. He's at Forward Aid. Why?"

"A few of the wounded have mentioned him. We were just curious," Anderson said.

"So, he's becoming a legend there?" I asked with a chuckle.

"Actually yes," Colby replied.

I'd save that juicy tidbit for our visit to the hospital ship.

28 April 1953

Dearest Mother and Dad,

You have probably already read about Operation Little Switch in the newspapers. My best buddy, Rawley Armstrong, may get his picture in the papers. They called him down to the office to meet with a war correspondent from the New York Times.

Anyway, since I know you like to do the Times' crossword puzzles together, I thought you could look for the picture. Would you cut out the articles and send them to me? I may be able to recognize some of the people.

Have you heard anything from Anthony Sarino's wife, Eloisa? I really hope that will work itself out for their sake.

I'm at a Forward Aid station where we patch up the men then send them to Able Med. We've only had a few minor injuries so we've had an easy time. These Marines are a tough bunch. I hardly have to do much. Well, I'm going to play cards with Fitzpatrick so I'll close for now.

All the love a son can give,

Orrin

CHAPTER FIFTEEN

29 April 1953

Dearest Mother and Dad,

It's hard to believe our neighbor's daughter little Darlene with freckles and pigtails is now old enough to get married. Wish her and the Lenardson clan well for me.

I just have to say how proud I am to be your son. To hire Eloisa Sarino at the VA hospital and let her and Isabella stay with you is absolutely wonderful. I know it will make her husband so happy. Yes, Mother, I realize now how hard it was to raise me with Dad a POW. All the same, I'm glad you came through for me.

The Marine Corps is in reserve now, which means all the Marines have been pulled off the line and are near Seoul to do some amphibian training. I'm happy they're getting a break.

The one thing though is Able Med is staying here in support of the KMCs, ROKs, and the U.S. Army. I don't mind so much. I receive combat pay which will add to my savings account. Don't worry, Mother. I'm not in actual combat; it's because I'm not back in reserve. Now that the Marines aren't fighting, we don't have too many casualties. Please write as often as you can.

All the love a son can give,

Orrin

ALTHOUGH THE MARINES WERE IN reserve, Able Med remained busy. Colonel Doerr, the commanding officer, invited the nearby Korean families in for checkups. The offer of a free meal in the mess tent brought in thirty.

The new Korean corpsman, Kim Lee, assisted and translated for me and Orrin as we directed the families to the proper area. Lee stayed with the large group outside while we tended to the children in a makeshift exam room in the ward.

A few of the children had infected farming injuries from cuts and scratches, even calluses from the hard work on the farm and in the rice paddies. Such a hard life for children so young. I wasn't sure this war would make things better for them no matter who came out on top.

Orrin cleaned a cut with antiseptic on the forearm of a seven-year-old boy. I took out an infected splinter in a grandfather's foot. Suddenly, an explosion outside vibrated the tent. All hell broke loose. Marines barked orders. The Koreans were yelling. Corpsman Kim Lee shouted back. Without scaring the boy, Orrin patted his head and helped him off the treatment table to join his mother beside him.

Carrying an unconscious girl, maybe age four, Kim Lee burst through the door. Blood covered Kim and the girl and created a red path. A distraught Korean man wrung his hands and rushed after them. Drs. James and Sinclair hurried toward the operating room.

I stopped Bob Waters. "What the hell happened?" I demanded.

"She was racing her brother and stepped on one of the landmines in the paddy field near the perimeter of camp," Waters said, shaken by the mishap. I shook my head and swore.

"She gonna make it?" Orrin asked.

"I don't know. She'll lose a leg for sure."

That put a damper on the rest of the morning. Keeping a close hand on their children, the parents lined up for lunch. Orrin, a few others, and I gathered our homemade sweets to share.

On the warm sunny spring day, the corpsmen and doctors taught the Korean children how to play baseball. A couple of Marines created a baseball diamond near the motor pool while most of the corpsmen paired up with the kids.

I taught a ten-year-old boy how to swing the bat on the sidelines. Fitzpatrick pitched underhand to the boy, who hit it toward third then ran that way. I pointed and ran with him to first base. Always angry, Fitz actually laughed.

Soon the kids and Marines were having fun. Orrin cheered from the sideline with their parents. For a moment, I forgot where I was. Marines reverted to the innocence of their youth. Not that many years ago for most.

When the P.A System cracked on, the illusion was suddenly broken. The men tensed at the anticipated announcement. I saw Orrin wince, too.

"Colonel Doerr wants all personnel to fall in at the center of the compound," it said.

And just like that, the baseball game was forgotten.

General Berry from Battalion Reserve and Colonel Doerr stood in front of the three rows of Marines. Unsure what to do, the Korean parents warily stood in the shadows of the tents.

"Corpsmen Connor and Armstrong, front and center," Doerr bellowed.

Surprised, Orrin and I strode stiffly toward the officers.

General Berry stepped forward with two small gray boxes. "We are here to present Hospital Corpsman 3rd Class Orrin Connor and Hospital Corpsman 3rd Class Rawley Armstrong the 'Letter of Commendation' Medal with the Combat 'V' for heroic service in the line of their profession while serving with a Marine infantry company during the operations against the enemy in Korea on 21 March 1953, displaying courage and professional skill."

He pinned the medal on me and then on Orrin.

"Thank you, sir," we replied.

Validation for our bravery and skills. I've come a long way from treating common ailments with Grandma's herbal medicine to treating life-threatening wounds in combat. I think she'd be proud.

"Your conduct throughout served as an inspiration to all who observed you, and was in keeping with the highest traditions of the United States Naval Service."

He saluted us. We returned it. After he dismissed the group, the Marines cheered and congratulated us. Smiling, I shook hands and accepted the kudos. Orrin quietly nodded.

"The first of many more, boys," I teased.

Orrin slipped away to our tent. From the doorway, I watched him put his medal back in its box, then toss it into the trash.

I frowned. "Why the hell did you do that? You earned it."

"I don't want it," Orrin replied.

"Why? You got something good to write home about."

Orrin shook his head. "I don't want to tell the story about how I got it. It's horrifying. Every time I look at it, I'd be reminded of the men who died." Preventing any further discussion, Orrin left the tent.

He had a point.

3 May 1953

Dearest Mother and Dad,

How are you doing tonight? How is spring in Amarillo? Rawley said back at his home, May brings the uplifting scent of lilacs. He and his sister love the vibrant green of the new grass and leaves. Sounds heavenly to me.

We played baseball with the young children from a nearby village. Today was a beautiful spring day. Not a care in the world. It was nice to hear the children and corpsmen laughing.

I bought a $1 chance ticket on a weekend trip to Seoul today. The money goes to a Korean family whose young daughter was hurt.

I met a Korean corpsman named Kim Lee. He is able to speak a little English and is hoping to go to school in the States. He went to corps school in Pusan and really knows his medicine. He is teaching us Korean while we help him learn English.

Boy, I sure wish they could get the truce talks over with so we may all go home.

All the love a son can give,

Orrin

CHAPTER SIXTEEN

10 May 1953

Dearest Mother and Dad,

Yes, Mother, I did receive a "Letter of Commendation" Medal. So did my buddy, Rawley. Well, it was stolen the same day I got it. That's why I didn't mention it. I am very sorry you got an official military letter thinking it was a death notification. I didn't mean for that to happen.

You said in your last letter that three thousand Marines landed at San Francisco. That was the twenty-first and twenty-second draft returning. Maybe next time, the twenty-third and twenty-fourth will go home. Then the next month, the twenty-fifth and twenty-fifth-and-a-half drafts, then the twenty-sixth, and then finally, the twenty-seventh draft will go home. That is the one I am in. So you see, it will probably be a few more months. It will either be September or October. I'll let you know for sure when the twenty-sixth leaves. We will be next.

Now that the Marines aren't on the lines fighting, we don't have any wounded. The only ones we're taking care of now are the 11th Marines. They are the artillery and never have any casualties. When we return, I hope I'll find a letter from you.

All the love a son can give,

Orrin

FLYING DOWN THE ROAD, ORRIN drove me and the newest addition to Able Med, Corpsman Kollen Kunesh, who had yet to receive a nickname. Kunesh had been at Battalion Reserve away from the fighting since he arrived with us back in December.

Smiling while flooring it, Orrin bounced the jeep toward the 11th Marines camp northwest of Able Med close to the MLR. We would hold sick call for a couple days, check everyone's feet, and tend to minor ailments. We looked forward to the mundane, hoping the truce talks would be a positive outcome.

At the first checkpoint, two Marines approached our jeep from behind the barrier of two saw horses. "Where you headed?" the biggest one asked.

"Just sightseeing," I replied.

"You know the Chinese are on the other side of that hill," the biggest one said, pointing to the hill about two miles from them.

I rolled my eyes and held up my medical bag. "Heading to your 11th."

With a hand motion to the smaller Marine to move the barrier aside, he lowered his voice. "Hey, before you go, could you help me with an issue?"

I pointed to Kunesh, who then followed the Marine twenty yards away from the road. Five minutes later, Kunesh returned failing to keep a neutral expression on his face. He either looked disgusted or constipated, hard to tell. He quickly hopped into our jeep.

"Let's get the hell away from here," Kunish said under his breath.

"Crabs, a rash, or the clap?" I asked, smiling at his discomfort.

"Let's just say I gave him a shot of penicillin and leave it at that. He said he got back from Seoul a week ago."

"That's gross," Orrin replied. "Those girls aren't regulated by the government."

"The ones in Japan are," I said.

"Will I get to go to Japan?" Kunesh asked, leaning forward.

"Us first," I replied. "We've got MLR seniority." I made that up, but it should be a rule.

Orrin continued down the bumpy two-track. "I miss the straight flat roads back home. I reached eighty once. The poor car had shaken so violently that the fender fell off," Orrin said, smiling as he reminisced on a more carefree time.

Outside the 11th Marines' camp, Orrin stopped at another checkpoint next to abandoned huts destroyed by artillery earlier in the war. The large sign just beyond the Marines standing guard had large words in Korean and slightly smaller words in English: NO CIVILIANS. NO REFUGEES. NO CHILDREN. TRESPASS AND DIE.

"State your business," the bulky Marine demanded. His arms were as big as Kunesh's torso.

We swallowed at the intimidating stare. No wonder he had this job. We had a legitimate reason to be here and even I was terrified of the guy.

"Uh, we're corpsmen from Able Med. Here for sick call," Orrin stammered.

"Right. We're expecting you," he said, with a smile. A creepy smile. "Hey, before you head in, can I talk to one of you?"

Orrin and I looked at Kunesh in the backseat. "My turn again?" Kunesh asked.

I thumbed for him to join the huge Marine beside the sign. With a sigh, he grabbed his medical bag. Five minutes later, Kunesh got back into the jeep. He didn't make eye contact with either of us. The men waved them through and pointed to the C.O.'s tent.

"On leave a week ago?" I asked him.

Kunesh blanched. "Whenever I get leave, I know what I'm not doing."

The camp close to the front had its guns facing every direction. In awe, the corpsmen stared at the 155 mm anti-tank weapon. Because of the Korean terrain of mountains, hills, and rice paddies, finding a place for artillery positions became tricky. During the early fighting at the Pusan perimeter, the distance for artillery was much closer at five hundred yards.

At this camp, guns were still pointed in all directions, something they also learned at the beginning of the war. The same for the large signs denying entrance. Children had entered with hand grenades and killed many.

Early on, the 11th Marines had targeted enemy mortars, machine guns, and artillery positions as well as enemy troops. For the past year, they supported patrols like blasting that enemy tunnel and huge gun. The war was fairly stationary now with fighting over outposts. With most of the Marines in reserve, we could relax slightly and maybe take a deep breath or two.

By the time we set up shop, a line had formed. As one, we groaned. "They can't all have been on leave, right?" Kunesh asked.

"Let's hope not," Orrin replied.

"It seems to have become your specialty. How about 'Crabs' as a nickname?" I asked.

"Please, no."

With three screens and exam tables set up for semi-privacy, the corpsmen tended to the men. Most were minor. They all seemed to ignore an issue until it was red, puffy, painful, and infected. The corpsmen made sure to check everyone's feet. A few had the start of ingrown nails.

"You need to wear clean socks or that fungus will get worse," I said to the Marine in my cubby. Orrin chuckled from his area. It was the eighth straight time I'd said it. Orrin and Kunesh said it a few times, too.

During a lunch break, the corpsmen sat at a table in the corner of the mess tent. For being so close to the front, these guys had good hot chow.

While I complained about disgusting feet, Kunesh shook his head. "It's as if they shared the same prostitute."

I laughed. Orrin spit out his biscuit and pushed his tray away. Corporal Sims, with dark circles under his eyes indicating he was a seasoned Marine, sat down beside us. He opened his mouth, shut it, and then opened it again as if a fish out of water.

"What's your issue, Sims?" I asked.

"Uh, can I talk to the Vicar in private?" he asked, looking down at his meal.

Kunesh and I scrambled to the next table, still in earshot. Orrin turned to Sims. "What can I do for you?"

"Well, it's my buddy," he started. "Well, I heard you're a good listener. And, well, I'm worried about him."

"Does he need a doctor?"

"Uh, no. I don't want it on his medical record."

Orrin nodded. "What's your concern?"

"Well," he said, looking around. He lowered his voice. "We were with the 11th during the Battle of the Pusan Perimeter."

Sims shivered slightly as he remembered the horror. It was a blood bath with the enemy surrounding them. The reason the guns aimed in every direction, even now.

"During the Battle of Yongsan, we denied the communists access keeping the Pusan perimeter intact, but we lost so many men," Sims said. "Kent saw them die and saw the faces of the North Koreans we killed. We were in the thick of it. Hand to hand even."

"That would have been horrific for anyone," Orrin said.

"Maybe if he talked to someone unofficially, he'd feel better. With the truce talks back on and the Marines in reserve, I'm hoping we'll go home soon."

"I hope for that, too. Where can I find him?"

"He's in supply."

"I don't know what good I can do," Orrin said.

"It couldn't hurt. Thanks," Sims replied, standing with his tray still full of food.

Outside the compound, I tagged along with Orrin. Another Marine stopped us. "Hey, want in on the raffle? Twenty-five cents for a ticket. The winner gets the two millionth casing of this damn war. Tonight the winner's drawn."

"Why would I want that?" I asked.

"The money raised goes to the Marine War Memorial Fund."

"You should have started with that," Orrin said, pulling out his wallet. He handed him ten dollars. I gave him ten as well.

Stuffing our tickets into our pockets, we walked toward supply across the compound. When the P.A. System cracked on, we hesitated. Expecting an "Incoming wounded", we cringed. My stomach clenched into a tight ball.

"Marines are heading back to the front. Truce talks unsuccessful," it said.

That news made me want to vomit. Hope suddenly gone. The camp morale popped like a balloon. Every man we passed hung his head, either praying or cursing.

At the entrance to the supply tent, men shouted from inside. Alert, we flew through the opening toward the commotion. I guess being on the MLR ingrained it in us to run toward danger. Who knew I could be so brave?

Someone said, "No. Don't!"

"Everybody out!" someone else roared.

We rushed past the Marines exiting the tent and stopped just as Kent pulled the trigger to the gun in his mouth. Blood and brain matter sprayed the ammo crates behind him.

The sergeant herded the rest of the Marines out. Left with the body, Orrin and I covered him with my coat. Too late to help.

"Damn war," Orrin said.

"One second you're alive; the next you're not," I replied.

"What do you need, corpsmen?" the sergeant asked from behind us.

"A litter. We'll take him back to Able Med with us," Orrin said.

"Thank you," the sergeant replied.

15 May 1953

Dearest Mother and Dad,

One of the corpsmen, Fitzpatrick, is teaching me how to play bridge. I'm not very good yet, but I'm practicing on our down time. I should be pretty good by the time I get home. Mother, maybe I can play a hand or two with you and your bridge club.

I thought I would get to go to Japan in the next few days, but they said it would be a few more months. I'll write and let you know. I'm hoping to call. I miss the sound of your voice. Boy, I'm more than ready to go home.

All the love a son can give,

Orrin

CHAPTER SEVENTEEN

28 May 1953

Dearest Mother and Dad,

How is everything with you tonight? I think about you and Dad all the time. Did Cousin Johnny get his arm cast off yet? Does he still want to ride his bike? I bet he won't go down that hill so fast next time. I miss those bike riding days. It's too bad I didn't have a big hill near us growing up. I may have sped down the hill, too.

Anyway, we received our netting to put up around our cots. It's getting summer over here and the mosquitoes are pretty bad after all this rain. We've had a lot of leaks in almost all the buildings. I'd trip over a pail of water every two feet if I wasn't careful. I'll write more later.

All the love a son can give,
Orrin

IN ONE OF ABLE MED'S wards, I bandaged a Marine's thigh and helped him with his pants. Orrin set a pair of crutches next to Lieutenant Vance as he sat up in his cot. A few of the other Marines were in different stages of dress.

"As soon as the bus arrives, you and the rest of the wounded are heading to Battalion Reserve," Orrin said.

"Today?" Vance asked.

Orrin nodded and moved toward Private Gaines, who struggled to tie his boots one-handed. His arm in a sling would need major rehab from the bullet that nicked an artery. He could move his fingers though, so that was a start.

"Are you ready to go home?" Orrin asked while he tied Gaines' boots for him.

"I hope so. I've changed."

"We all have."

Before Orrin could say more to reassure him, a crash in the compound got our attention. Grabbing our guns leaning against the wall with the other corpsmen's, we hurried toward the noise. One of the buses that would take the wounded to Reserve had sideswiped the other, tipping them both on their sides.

"Are they empty?" Colonel Doerr asked.

"Yes, but both drivers are dead," Fitzpatrick said.

The colonel pointed and motioned for two corpsmen to take out the drivers. "Let's go, Marines!"

Five men turned them upright.

"Who can drive a bus?" Doerr asked the group.

"Armstrong and I can," Orrin said. I glanced at him. We never volunteer.

Doerr nodded. "Let's see if they start."

They ran a little rough with loud exhausts but still functional.

"Pack overnighters while I get your orders." Doerr turned away. "Get those wounded Marines on board," he said to no one in particular.

Orrin and I quickly packed a light bag. "I wonder how long we get to stay," I said.

We yearned for a break. The corpsmen turnaround kept us at Able Med. We liked that it padded our savings accounts, which kept us focused on our futures.

At the buses, Doerr handed us the wounded roster for each bus, and our orders, not that we needed papers. It was pretty obvious where we were going, but paperwork ran the military.

"Back in a week?" I asked.

"Nice try. Tomorrow," Doerr replied. "We need those buses for casualties. Something big is going down soon."

"Yes sir," Orrin said.

"Take it slow with the wounded," Doerr said, looking directly at Orrin, who blushed. The Vicar had a reputation as a speeder. He had once peeled out from the compound, sending dirt and dust into the C.O.'s office. He had to clean the whole area when he got back. It was painful to watch a slob try to be neat. It just wasn't in his nature.

On the second bus, Orrin made sure everyone was secure, a tight fit at capacity with twelve each with their own stretcher to relax. This would be a long ride, four hours if not longer, depending on the roads.

My bus chugged as Orrin followed me. He couldn't go fast now. I chuckled. Orrin once told me I drove like his mother, slow and deliberate. This was my payback. I bet he's rolling his eyes that I was in the first bus.

Halfway to Reserve, a billow of smoke came from my engine. "Oh, boy," I mumbled.

I jumped out, opened the hood, and stared at the smoking engine. Orrin joined me. I could tweak my truck but not this monster.

"Kaput," I said. "I guess we're riding with you."

Orrin nodded with a sinister smile. I laughed. We were an even tighter fit with twenty-two wounded. Four needed their own stretcher, the rest crammed in every which way. Responsible for so many, Orrin drove slowly while I checked on the more seriously injured Marines. Many grumbled about our sardine can arrangement.

"Hey, relax, fellas," I said. "We're getting farther from the front. Some of yous are going home, but the rest get at least a two-week vacation. So, who brought snacks?" The men shook their heads. "I bet the Vicar did."

Orrin smiled. "In my bag."

I dug around the bottom. "I knew you would share."

"What kind of road trip would this be if I didn't?"

"A boring one," I replied as I pulled out a large package.

"My mother sent me three batches of fudge and caramel popcorn to share. Eloisa helped her make it, so it's pretty tasty."

I gave each man an equal share. For the next two hours, I was the one who talked with the men about home. The time flew. I understood now why Orrin enjoyed it. A distraction from our circumstances.

Orrin slowed toward the gate that had a giant sign like the one at the 11th Marines' Artillery camp. Ahead of us, a child, maybe age six, approached the gate. From a distance, a Korean woman shouted and ran toward the boy and gate. Security yelled for him to stop. The child must not have understood because he kept walking.

One guard aimed his weapon, then shot him. The wounded on the bus watched helplessly as the child fell from the buckshot. Another Marine swooped in, checked him for weapons, then carried him into the compound for medical treatment. Alive, the child was back far enough that the wounds looked superficial. Thank God. The mother shrieked and was held back by a guard so she couldn't enter.

A few men on the bus screamed obscenities. Others cried. Just what we needed—more nightmares. All of us had been traumatized more than necessary over the course of this war.

The group tensed as Orrin stopped at the gate. I stepped down and handed the guard, who had shot the boy, our paperwork. "The other bus broke down," I said.

He shook his head.

I raised my voice. "Listen, buddy. I know you're security. Just let us through. We're all tired and hot. These boys were wounded on the front. You ever been there?" I asked, annoyed by the guard's pristine uniform and fresh haircut. Not to mention, he'd just shot a child and showed no remorse.

Orrin jumped out of the driver's seat. "What's the problem?" he asked as my temper escalated.

"Your paperwork says two buses," the guard replied.

Orrin nodded. "The other broke down."

"I told him that," I added.

Using his crutch, Lieutenant Vance hobbled down the bus steps. The guard snapped to attention. "Who's your superior?" Vance asked.

"Major Dern, sir," the guard replied.

"Would he want these wounded men reinjured because you wouldn't let them into the Reserve Hospital?"

"No sir, but—"

As one, we turned toward the rumbling of a general's jeep that stopped behind us. He, too, wanted inside the compound.

"Do I need to discuss this with the general?" Vance asked.

The guard's armpits were suddenly wet. "No sir." He motioned for the gate to open.

Vance limped back to the bus. Orrin helped him up the steps. "Thank you, sir," Orrin said.

"Thanks for sharing your fudge. It tasted like my wife's recipe. It felt like home wasn't that far away."

After supervising the care of the wounded with the battalion corpsmen, Orrin and I dropped off the bus to the motor pool. Then we found the large mess tent. The smell of chicken and dumplings overwhelmed our senses. I was lightheaded and my stomach growled.

"I feel underdressed," I said in the long line. We were the only two who had dusty clothes, sweaty bodies, and unshaven faces. The rest looked like the security guard.

"We'll find the showers after we eat," Orrin replied.

At the end of a table, we wolfed down our chow as if someone would take away our trays before we finished.

"The best meal I've had in months," Orrin said.

I nodded as I stuffed half a slice of bread in my mouth. Three Marines sat down beside us. The young men who maybe shaved once a month had an excited newness to their grins. Another annoyance.

"You come from the MLR?" one asked.

"Yes," Orrin said. Sipping his hot coffee, he closed his eyes. I savored the brew's flavor, too. Not thick and burnt like we were used to.

"Yeah, the coffee's mud around here," the other one said.

"It's not so bad," Orrin replied.

"So, what's it like? I mean, have you killed any gooks? We head up in two days."

I glanced at his young face. Were we ever that naïve about war? Maybe, but we changed quickly. Those three obviously hadn't been there yet. I didn't want to discuss our experiences. I knew Orrin didn't want to, either. In awe of war, these boys didn't understand, just like everyone back home. More than half of all Americans didn't even know where Korea was.

"You think we want to talk about that hell?" I asked, raising my voice.

"What's the big deal?"

Orrin rose from the bench and picked up his tray. Glaring, I stood up, too.

"Let's go," Orrin said. His anger, too, had escalated. I knew this because his neck and face got patchy red.

"Yeah, run away, worthless squids," the young knucklehead said.

Orrin tripped, sending his tray into the Marine's chest. Creamed corn dripped down onto his lap.

"I'm so sorry," Orrin said. His smirk surprised me. My jaw dropped.

The boy jumped up. The mess slid farther down his pressed pants. "Like hell. You did that on purpose."

I would have been more amused that Orrin started a fight for a change, but I was afraid he'd get thrown into the brig. Sergeant Martinez stomped over before our tussle got out of hand.

"What the hell is going on?" Martinez demanded.

"We just drove the wounded here from Able Med. I was tired and I tripped," Orrin said. I nodded.

"When do you go back?" Martinez asked.

"Tomorrow morning," Orrin replied.

Martinez nodded. "Hit the showers then the sack."

"But sir," the young Marine said.

"I'm not a sir, private. It was an accident. That's the end of it. Understood?"

"Yes si—yes."

Orrin quickly left. Once outside the door, I laughed.

It had been months since we had a hot shower. I groaned with relief. The water washed away my stress. I heard Orrin whisper his pep talk. "Buck up, man. Show no emotion. The men you care for count on you." Suddenly, my delight returned to despair for my friend.

We fell into spare bunks and slept until the commotion. The other men complained about the hell they were in. Life was relative, I guess.

"First chow, then I want to check on our guys before we leave," Orrin said, putting on his boots. It was the first time we'd slept with our boots off while over here. Truthfully, I thought I'd enjoy it. Instead, I felt exposed and vulnerable.

After powdered scrambled eggs and sausage, we walked into the ward. We shook a few hands and wished them luck.

"Hey, Vicar," Private Gaines said. "Do you think people will understand what we went through over here?"

Orrin sat on the stool beside him. How would Orrin answer that without Gaines losing hope? I'd like to know, too.

"Maybe in time," Orrin said.

He was a really good liar. I agreed with Orrin that Americans would forget, if they ever knew at all. Was I right, though? Would telling the truth about our experiences help? All I knew was that it helped me cope.

We stopped at the supply tent and made a pile of medical supplies we knew we needed or were running low on.

"Whatever you guys want. I heard that the Chinese and North Koreans are going to attack, hoping to gain extra territory to strengthen their position in the final armistice terms," Sergeant Martinez said.

"Damn commies," I mumbled.

Martinez threw in a case of candy bars. I tried to bargain for the whiskey but it was saved for a one-star general. Instead, he gave us a popcorn maker with thirty pounds of kernels, and two gallons of oil. Butter was a no-go, but we now had popcorn for movie night.

"Got any games?" Orrin asked. "It may distract the wounded in the recovery wards."

"I have puzzles," Martinez said.

"Great. Thank you," Orrin replied.

With fifteen jigsaw puzzles, we lugged all our booty to the motor pool to pick up our bus.

A corporal covered in grease and grime shook his head. "Oh, hey, we scrapped out your bus. I'm seriously surprised you made it here in one piece."

"What are we supposed to take back?" I asked, setting my pile on the ground.

"Oh yeah, well, we're giving you Easy Med's bus since they aren't ready for wounded yet."

"Why aren't they ready?" Orrin asked.

"All the med stations got pulled back when the Marines went into reserves. They're not set up yet. Able Med's the only hospital up there right now."

Shit, we'd be needed soon. "Keys?" I asked.

The corporal pointed to the clean bus, no scratches or dings. We quickly packed our supplies and headed out. Orrin floored it past the gate. I saluted the same guard as yesterday. As the dirt kicked up behind us, I laughed. Covered in dust, the guard flipped us the bird.

"Did you do that on purpose?" I asked.

"Do what?"

"I am really rubbing off on you."

"I think so," Orrin replied.

I looked around our new bus that would transport our wounded. "Does Able Med get all the shit equipment?"

"Good thing we're the best at what we do."

"Damn right," I replied, settling in for the long drive back.

Luckily, we made it back before the casualties started. Colonel Doerr met us when we stopped inside the compound. He eyed the new bus.

"We brought extra supplies and a popcorn maker," I said. A few corpsmen gathered around to unpack.

"And popcorn?" Doerr asked.

I nodded but bit my tongue at the dumb Doerr question. Of course, we brought popcorn, too. What a knucklehead!

"Great!" Fitzpatrick smiled. "Tonight's movie night."

The smell of popcorn filled the mess tent where the projector and screen had been set up. I accepted the praise for my awesome trading skills. I enjoyed being the hero. As everyone settled in with their full bags of salty goodness, the P.A. System cracked on.

"Incoming wounded."

Everyone crammed as much popcorn into their mouths as they could, then left to prepare for casualties. Orrin had a quick minute to write a letter. Who knew when he'd get another chance?

29 May 1953

Dearest Mother and Dad,

Just a short letter. The movie wasn't any good tonight, but the popcorn was delicious. The Marines have gone back up to the front again. Please say a prayer or two for them.

All the love a son can give,

Orrin

CHAPTER EIGHTEEN

20 June 1953

Dearest Mother and Dad,

I read in the Stars and Stripes that Ethel and Julius Rosenberg were executed for espionage yesterday for passing information about the atomic bomb to the Soviet Union. I'm sorry, Mother, but I think they deserved to die. I hate the thought of another war. These Marines need a break. We all want to go home.

As I sit and write this letter, I can hear a lot of fighting going on up on the line. Sounds like big artillery to me. When I first arrived here, I couldn't tell one type of artillery from another, but after being over here for a time I can almost call every round. When we start throwing heavy gear, Able Med had better stand by.

Thank you for the sweets and batteries for my flashlight. Batteries are always needed and hardly ever available. I'll send more pictures home in the next letter.

All the love a son can give,

Orrin

BOOM! MORTAR FIRE SHOOK THE Forward Aid bunker. Working at a makeshift operating table with my flashlight resting on the Marine's legs, I leaned over the abdominal wound so the raining dust from the sandbags wouldn't contaminate it. I packed it off the best I could.

Corpsman Bob Waters came in to load the Marine onto the helicopter. "Rawley, who else?"

"Michaels," I said, pointing to the Marine with a shattered leg. More than likely it would have to be amputated.

The battle on Heady Hill had brought in seven wounded already. More on the way. Taking a deep breath, Waters and I carried the Marine with an abdominal wound then the one with the shattered leg to the helicopter. As it took off, the bus arrived for the rest.

Our new bus had bullet holes across the right side from a sniper. Dirt and blood covered the interior. I didn't think Easy Med would want it back in its present condition.

When more wounded arrived, I focused on the task at hand and quickly washed my hands, getting back to work. I prayed for my friend's safety. Orrin had drawn the short straw for patrol this time.

At 0500, the artillery lessened until it was quiet. Then there were cries of pain. Twenty-seven Marines had come through this Forward Aid station. I hadn't seen Orrin with any of them. I waited and evacuated the last of the wounded. The fighting was done for now. Did they protect Heady? Who really cared?

I grabbed my carbine, medical bag, and a rolled-up litter. "I'm heading up there for any KIA or WIA." Waters seemed relieved not to have to go. "When the bus gets back, send two corpsmen and another litter."

I followed the trail the Marines had used to the front of Heady and the trench system. Using the natural terrain, I stopped beside a couple of Marines with minor injuries. I treated them and they stayed at their post.

"Did you notice anyone else out here?" I whispered.

"The main trench this side of the command bunker."

I nodded in the bare hint of daylight. Along the trench, I found Private Thomas with a shoulder wound and another dead for not keeping his damn head down. Living first.

"Anyone else?" I asked as I bandaged his shoulder.

Thomas pointed over the trench wall. I peeked over the side to the valley below and spotted three Marines.

"Are you able to cover me?" I asked.

He nodded then put his carbine on the trench wall. With my gun and bag slung over my shoulder, I climbed over the side and slid down the rocky terrain. The move was so loud I thought it echoed between the two hills.

Knowing the enemy liked taking pot shots, I crept toward them and spotted Orrin. My heart was in my throat when Orrin didn't move. As I got closer, Orrin looked back and waved. I checked for a pulse on one of the Marines.

"He's dead. A bullet made a nice hole through the neck," Orrin whispered. When Orrin's sarcasm increased, it meant his anxiety level had, too. He pressed on the other Marine's abdomen. "See who we got here? Private What's-it-like-on-the-front."

Sure enough. The Marine Orrin had tripped into with his food tray at the Reserve Hospital lay wounded.

"I got another litter on the way and cover at the trench," I said, looking around.

"That ass Thomas? He's the one that hit the dead guy," Orrin said.

"Damn. As if we need to worry about friendly fire now," I replied.

As one, we carried the private upward to the trench cut into the hill. By the time we reached it, two corpsmen helped lift him over and carried him on a litter to Forward Aid.

I ripped the gun out of Thomas's hands. "You help Connor while I cover you."

With his head down, Thomas followed Orrin to get the KIA. I whispered a bunch of swear words. My friend could have died. Orrin picked up the dead Marine under the arms. Thomas lifted the man's legs but lost his balance and fell backward. He landed on a Bouncing Betty mine. It shot shrapnel and his body up and out in every direction.

The dead Marine in Orrin's arms took the brunt of metal. A piece winged Orrin in the upper arm next to his scar from his first patrol. Looking stunned, he stood there staring at the pieces of Thomas. A leg by the feet of the dead Marine. An arm ten feet away. Thomas's mangled torso in the hole the explosion had made.

"Get your ass down," I growled from the trench.

Orrin struggled to pull the dead Marine, who'd just saved his life, up the hill. We didn't even know his name. Once we were safe in the trench, I hugged my buddy. In the middle of Korea, Orrin gripped me back. That could have been Orrin. I blinked away my tears; Orrin did the same, our vulnerability raw. Too shaken to talk, we sat and waited until we stopped trembling.

"I'll go back and get him," Orrin whispered.

I took the litter and we carefully collected the pieces of Thomas. His family would want a proper burial. On the bus with the KIA, I tended to Orrin's flesh wound while Orrin drove slowly this time. The silence was broken when I patted his shoulder.

"The hand of God, my friend," I said with a sad chuckle. "That mine was buried only three feet away from you. That's a story for the campfire."

"Too scary," he replied. I agreed.

By 1800, the bus loads of wounded were settled in a ward or were shipped to the U.S.S. *Repose*, the hospital ship off Inchon. Although we were exhausted, an air of excitement filled Able Med. A USO show was set up in the mess tent. A needed distraction for the evening. Maybe the nightmares of the day would lessen. I hoped so.

With popcorn in a bag, Orrin sat in the middle row of benches. I joined him. We had met the three women and three men earlier as they visited with the wounded. Orrin had laughed as I tripped over myself trying to talk to the blonde singer. The first time I was tongue-tied with a girl. I must be out of practice.

"She's so beautiful," I said, staring longingly at her. I didn't care if she could sing or not.

When the announcer introduced the singers, the P.A. System cracked on. The whole room deflated with groans at the next message.

"Flash Red!" it said.

The compound darkened.

"Not tonight," I said.

Everyone scattered out of the mess, leaving the USO people dumbfounded. I walked up to them and motioned them off the temporary stage.

"Enemy planes are in the area. Follow me to the bunker." I reached out for the blonde's smooth hand. She smelled like roses.

Smiling, Orrin shook his head. While I showed our guests to the bunker, Orrin hurried to help the patients cram inside. Outside the crowded shelter, the corpsmen had our weapons ready. We weren't sure how good we'd be against an enemy bomb dropping from an airplane, but we looked tough and brave in front of the USO gals.

With an "all clear", the USO quickly packed up and left along with any morale Able Med had. In our tent, the corpsmen tried to relax after a disappointing day. To top it off, because of the scare, no mail was delivered. With a sigh, Orrin searched for a fresh piece of paper and listened to the chatter.

"We should just pull out and let them fight it out themselves," Waters said.

"Especially after all we've done for them," Fitzpatrick added.

"I don't think they could continue to fight for two weeks without our help," Waters said.

"Americans are dying. For what?" Kunesh said.

"The only reason they don't want us to leave is they're making too much money off us," Fitzpatrick replied.

"After the deal the South Koreans pulled by letting go of all the POWs, who knows if the next prisoner exchange will happen," Waters said.

"Gooks. All gooks," Fitzpatrick said.

I had enough. "Shut the hell up! It's not our choice. We do what we're told. Stop crying about it."

"Jeez, we're just letting off some steam," Fitzpatrick said, scowling.

21 June 1953

Dearest Mother and Dad,

We had another Flash Red which means enemy planes were in the area. You may have read in the papers or heard over the radio that the Chinese have dropped a few bombs on Seoul. The Chinese haven't bothered us any, but we aren't taking any chances heading to the bunkers when there is one. So don't worry, Mother.

The USO came to Able Med. I sure wish they had more shows over here to boost morale. Rawley thinks he met the love of his life. He's the best friend a guy could ask for. A truly good man.

We have stuck close to our radios for the past few days in hopes they will end this war and we can go home. Another day gone and another day closer to seeing you both again. From the way things are over here, I don't think my draft will leave until sometime in October. I am pretty sure it won't be any later.

All the love a son can give,
Orrin

CHAPTER NINETEEN

7 July 1953

Dearest Mother and Dad,

I'm sorry I haven't written. I ran out of paper and it's at a premium over here. So imagine my surprise to open your package to find stationery. Thank you.

I shared your treats with the wounded in our ward. It cheers them right up. It's like magic medicine.

Yes, Mother, I've learned so much about surgery here. It will help me get into medical school I'm sure. I don't know which university I want to attend yet. I still have time to decide.

Enjoy your trip to Minneapolis. It should be the perfect weather way up north. Please thank your bridge club for the letters of encouragement to the corpsmen at Able. We appreciate their prayers.

Since the Marines went back on the line, Able Med has been the only Evac hospital in operation until C, E, and B Meds get back to their old positions. Able Med is elite. We can handle anything the North Koreans and Chinese throw at us.

All the love a son can give,
Orrin

AT 2100, THE P.A. SYSTEM announced for the second time that the Chinese hit Outpost Berlin and casualties were on the way. In the middle of the compound, Orrin and I rushed to Dr. Sinclair, the big burly doctor, who had waved us over.

"I want you both to supervise the priority order of the wounded coming in," Sinclair said.

We nodded. We had done it before but were expecting many casualties tonight. We usually just had Dr. Arrogant helping us. This time, every doctor would be in surgery.

"I want Kunesh and Fitzpatrick to tend to the minor wounds. The rest of the corpsmen will keep an eye on those waiting for surgery," Dr. Sinclair said, before disappearing.

We relayed his orders and rushed to the helicopter pad for the first arrivals. We knew the corpsmen at the Forward Aid Stations shipped the high priority first.

Night turned into day as the casualties continued to arrive. With any break in the action, the corpsmen moved and organized the wounded in the tight-fitting wards. Those that were ambulatory were taken somewhere toward the rear for care.

Taking a deep breath at 1800, we looked around. We stood in the center of wounded men on litters scattered all over the ground waiting for surgery. It made me dizzy as I took in the panoramic view. The heat on the overcast day didn't help the men. Wounds flowed and blood soaked into the ground.

"God, please end this hell," Orrin mumbled.

"Vicar," a wounded Marine whispered.

Orrin looked down. Anthony "Turq" Sarino had a knife wound to his abdomen. Orrin knelt beside him and checked his bandage. "Rawley," he shouted and waved. "He's next."

I yelled at Kunish and pointed.

"You have pull here?" Turq said weakly.

"I do. We'll fix you right up." Orrin said.

"Listen. I lost my good luck stone. If I die, let my girls know I loved them with all my heart."

"Hey. I gotta get you home. I want my bedroom back from Isabella. She's probably got all kinds of dolls in it."

Turq smiled. "Thank your parents for making them part of your family."

"You can thank them yourself," Orrin said as Kunesh and I picked up his litter to take him to surgery.

At 2200, on a break before the next wave of wounded were brought in, I carried around a tray of orange juice. With no time to eat, it gave us a boost. Orrin downed it in one swallow.

"Turq didn't make it," I said.

Sadness for his girls overwhelmed us. Life was not fair. It made no sense. As Orrin processed the loss, Colonel Doerr joined us. He took a glass of juice.

The P.A. System announced, "Incoming in fifteen minutes."

"We can sleep when we're dead," Doerr said before walking away.

"Sleep well, Turq," Orrin whispered.

Two hundred and fifty wounded Marines and Army soldiers came through Able Med. Orrin and I remained on duty to care for the men in the ward while the other corpsmen got some needed sleep. In a daze, I sat at the table and rubbed my hands over my face. Most of the men slept after their stressful ordeal. Orrin set a mug of coffee in front of me then sat down.

On the other side of the ward, an Army soldier with a broken leg and a Marine with his arm in a sling mumbled to each other. The whispers escalated into shouting. Orrin rushed over. I was too tired to follow. I could easily hear them from here.

"Damn Army needs the Marines to do their job!" Marine Sergeant Joseph Zims said.

"Screw you. We've been fighting the war long before you got here," Army Sergeant Steven Randall replied.

"Yeah, 'cause you couldn't finish it."

They both sat up at the same time. The soldier's leg in the cast swung around and hit the Marine in the head.

"I just finished it," Randall replied, with a smile.

"Hey!" Orrin said in a loud whisper. "Knock it off!"

"A love tap," Zims said. "Can't even do that right."

The two big guys started pushing and shoving each other without actually standing. With a one-foot gap between beds, it was easy. They ignored Orrin and their swings got harder as their adrenaline returned.

Hearing the commotion, Dr. Sinclair, bigger than both, came over to help separate them. Randall's leg cast swung around and hit Zims's shoulder. Both howled in pain.

"Stop it right now!" Sinclair demanded.

The fight abruptly ended. Either the doctor had a little more pull then a lowly corpsman squid, or they were now in pain and glad to have a reason to stop.

"Let's get these asses to x-ray," Sinclair said to Orrin and me. He turned back to the men. "If you wake any of these other boys, I'll put you on report."

Orrin found a wheelchair for Randall and Dr. Sinclair helped Zims. Amused, I followed. With a black eye, Sergeant Zims had torn the stitches in his shoulder, so I tended to him while Sinclair and Orrin x-rayed Randall's leg. As Sinclair looked over the x-rays in the other room, Orrin sat on the stool.

Steven Randall lay back on the wooden exam table. Exhaustion finally hit him. "Such a bloody fight on Berlin," Randall mumbled.

"Why continue it here?" Orrin asked.

"He doesn't understand." Randall turned his head and looked at Orrin. "I've been fighting over here for a year. Killing men at hand to hand combat. We don't have a choice. We just do it."

"Great men know they have a choice, but they choose not to have one for the greater good of their country," Orrin said.

Randall smiled. "Did Navy just call the Army great?"

"What? No. Do you have a concussion?" Orrin asked. Randall snorted.

Carrying the x-ray film, Dr. Sinclair returned to the room. "You reinjured it so we have to put on a new cast," the doctor said to the Army sergeant.

On the way back to the recovery ward, the Marine laughed. "Army loser."

That started another fight. In his broken cast, Randall jumped up and went after Zims. They crashed backward into the x-ray table, smashing it. Orrin stepped forward to break them up.

Sinclair held up his hand to stop him. "They'll tire out soon enough. Get some help and separate them."

Rolling on the floor, they smacked each other until they collapsed. Three more corpsmen helped them to cots at the ends of the ward.

It seemed frustration with the war had taken over every branch of the military.

14 July 1953

Dearest Mother and Dad,

We just got a brand-new x-ray table. We took the old one down. It's surprising how you can pack a large table into such a small box.

Mother, I can go all day thinking about a million things to write home about, but when I get a chance to settle down and write, I can't think of a thing.

Please give Eloisa my condolences. I was with Anthony before he died. He appreciated you taking his girls under your wing. He wanted them to know how much he loved them. Enclosed is a group picture of Sarino and some of the corpsmen the first time we met him. He was a good man and brave Marine.

I found that mail from you is the most important thing in the day. Please keep up the good writing. It sure makes the time until I go home shorter.

All the love a son can give,

Orrin

CHAPTER TWENTY

25 July 1953

Dearest Mother and Dad,

It has rained almost five inches, and it's still coming down. The showers near the rice paddies flooded and washed away all our clothes that we left to be laundered by the locals. Even the tent washed away. You should have seen ten Marines chasing after the clothes and tent. They could have had a nice swim in the rice paddy lake if they weren't in their dungarees and boots. I took a few pictures.

I guess it would be just about seventy more days and I'll board a ship for home. The thing that worries me is if they do sign the truce, will they keep up with the rotation for the drafts going home? I sure hope they sign though.

All the love a son can give,

Orrin

AT 0100 IN THE COMMAND post bunker, Orrin tucked his letter and pencil into his pocket. Next to him, I signed mine to my sister. Orrin still saw no sense in telling his family anything about his experiences. It was about the only thing we disagreed on. It gave me peace to share. Orrin said he found solace in not worrying his family. I thought it wasn't worry that my sister would take from it but an understanding about the effect the war was having on us.

While waiting for the 11th Marines to start the artillery fire on the enemy position, Orrin and I watched Major Ainsworth discuss strategy with his officers who would take charge of the men in their platoons. This battle had two hundred Marines positioned along the trench ready for the command to attack. Orrin, Kunesh, Waters, and I would disperse throughout the areas.

The humid rain pounded in the darkness—the case whenever we were on patrol. We could walk right past the enemy. I shivered slightly; the enemy could walk right up to us.

Water dripped from the sandbags above us. Would that wet sand withstand a direct hit? I didn't want to be inside to find out. There were no safe places anywhere.

On schedule at 0130, the 11th lit up the area. I hoped it would take out all the North Koreans and Chinese so we could go back to Able. We'd soon find out.

The corpsmen followed the men out of the bunker. Orrin and I crept to the left in the trench, Kunesh and Waters to the right. Hot and sweaty inside our raingear, Orrin and I stayed close together. This would be an offensive battle, not a defensive patrol that we were used to doing. How different would it be?

The heavy rain had canceled our air support. We depended on the 11th and their adjusted calculations to hit the enemy hill. Orrin and I slogged behind the men toward the downhill communication trenches flanking our own hill position.

With two platoons, Orrin and I trudged closer to the MLR. In the rain and darkness, I barely saw the Marine in front of me. Forming a daisy chain of our hand on the shoulder of the Marine in front of us gave me a bit of comfort that I wasn't alone. The mortar flashed a beacon to get us moving down the trench system.

At the ready to climb out of the trench and cross the valley, the Marines remained quiet. Not that it mattered. I didn't hear the sergeant yell for the Marines to start until the man in front of me moved. We jogged downslope through the river of rain that beat us to the valley.

The mortar fire—theirs and ours, depending on who had the area at the time—flattened the end of the trench. With our carbines, Orrin and I stooped low and sidestepped the drainage of mud. At the first sound of burp guns, five South Korean soldiers retreated. I had heard ROK soldiers would run away, too afraid to fight. To actually see it angered me. The Marines were fighting for them.

Orrin yelled for the young Marine in front of him to get down. When the man turned, a bullet hit him in the head, dropping him into the running water. Dead. I aimed my gun in the direction I thought the shot had come from. I saw nothing in the darkness.

Wiping my face of rain, I cautiously worked my way toward the Marines, Orrin farther in front. Where were they? Feeling alone in the downpour, I pushed forward. An explosion lit the area to my left. A Bouncing Betty killed two Marines and injured two others.

"Corpsman!"

Kneeling in the puddle of mud, Orrin checked the first wounded Marine. He plucked out the dog tags of the dead Marine that had lodged in the other's butt. I crawled toward Orrin.

"It's superficial. Can you still fight?" Orrin asked. The Marine nodded.

Orrin helped him to his knees. A bullet skimmed across Orrin's forehead before entering the Marine's skull. We dropped back into the mud. Blood and rain dripped into Orrin's eyes. Wiping his muddy hand on his pants, he swiped his forehead, feeling the graze. Anger replaced my fear for Orrin.

We crawled toward the flank where the bullet had come from, searching for Marines and the enemy. Our guns ready. A hand grabbed my leg, startling me. The sergeant was lying on the ground. This damn rain! I never even saw him. I yanked Orrin backward and pushed him down.

Lying side by side, the sergeant pointed through the flashes of mortar fire to the line of Chinese walking past us toward our trench three feet away. We carefully raised our guns. The sergeant shot first then the other Marines alongside us.

"Protect our flank!" the sergeant shouted.

In the darkness, we traded gunfire with the enemy—randomly shooting hoping to hit someone. Would it dwindle our ammo? I couldn't think about that right now. Orrin and I crawled toward an injured Marine as three more screamed for help. I bandaged the hand of the first one.

"I can still fight," he said.

I pointed him in the direction of the sergeant and the other Marines. Orrin and I met again at the next Marine shot in the knee. He wasn't going anywhere.

"Will I lose my leg?" he asked, cringing in evident pain.

"Not if I can help it." Orrin took the clip out of his carbine and bullet from the chamber. He used it to stabilize the knee, tying it off above and below the wound. "Can you cover us while we check on your buddy?" Orrin asked.

"Yes."

We crawled toward the third Marine, who'd been shot in the arm. We wrapped it and made him crawl closer to the one with the injured knee for protection. The fourth Marine, the youngest kid we'd seen so far, stared at us, the rain washing any dirt from his face. The terrified boy had three oozing chest wounds. The best we could do for him now was a shot of morphine.

The boy gripped Orrin's hand. "Don't leave me."

"I'm right here," Orrin said.

The Marine closed his eyes. His breathing shallowed as he struggled for a breath. This by far was the worst part of war—waiting for a man to die. Ten seconds later, the boy's hand slackened from Orrin's. Focus on the living! Orrin slung the strap of the dead boy's carbine over his shoulder. We'd come back for him later.

The rain finally let up and the clouds moved on. The moon shone its light throughout the valley, our dark reprieve gone. I wished it back. Orrin and I carried the Marine with the injured knee back to the trench. More men passed us, entering into the valley to reinforce our flank.

Coming across an injured man with a shoulder wound, Orrin quickly bandaged it and made him help the one with the knee wound to Forward Aid. Pausing at the end of the trench, we listened for Marines needing help. A Marine with a belly wound staggered toward us. I laid him down to look.

While I bandaged his wound, Orrin rested the dead boy's carbine on the top of the trench's sandbag wall. Out of the corner of my eye, I saw movement. More wounded Marines coming back? We were getting hammered. Three Chinese soldiers crept closer to the entrance of our trench. Orrin shot one, then the other. The gun jammed before Orrin could shoot the third. I couldn't react fast enough. The enemy aimed his weapon at us.

A shot rang out and the enemy soldier dropped. We looked back to see the Marine with the injured knee give us a thumbs-up at the top of the trench system above us. *Thank you.*

For another hour, Orrin and I took turns running onto the valley floor to give aid to the Marines while the other defended the end of the trench. From what I could tell, we hadn't gotten very far.

Out of one hundred Marines in the two platoons, we had helped seventy-five. I hoped the other corpsmen had better luck. Our supplies had run out, even the items we used to improvise.

Whoever was left returned to regroup. At the edge of the main trench higher up on the hill, Marines fired toward the center of the valley. Back at a defensive position, Kunesh met us and handed us fresh supplies. Orrin peeked over the trench wall into the flat in front of the command bunker. The Chinese crept slowly. None of the Marines from the trench above us saw them. The sandbag wall of the trench was too high to see just below them.

"Sergeant!" Orrin pointed to the enemy.

After a quick glance, the sergeant sent up a flare then motioned for the remaining Marines to shoot them, drawing the attention to the platoon up higher on the hill. In the light, I saw a Marine pinned down behind a rock, hidden from the enemy. I backtracked and quickly crawled toward him. The Marine had a broken lower leg. Part of the bone stuck out. I applied a splint.

In the trench above, Orrin pointed the sergeant to me and the Marine beside the rock. The Chinese in the center scattered and returned fire. I was about to be overrun with

Chinese. Before I knew it, Orrin crawled toward the rock twenty yards away.

"Damn it, Rawley. What are you doing?" Orrin whispered.

"Now you know how I felt. He's got a broken leg," I replied.

"I'm okay. I can fight," the Marine mumbled in shock. I shot him full of morphine.

"The sergeant knows we're here," Orrin said.

"I'll cover you. He's not that heavy to carry."

Orrin shook his head. "No, you're stronger."

In the distance, the sergeant roared, "Move it, Vicar!"

I heaved the man over my shoulder in a fireman's carry. Orrin shot two Chinese coming toward us. He had become soaked in red—figuratively and literally. He saved me—again.

27 July 1953

Dearest Mother and Dad,

The Marines were hit hard the other night. In a company of two hundred, only sixteen were left uninjured. We worked to help them for eighteen hours straight. Not to worry, we were safely stationed at Able

Med at the time. The Marines hadn't made much ground though.

How are Eloisa and Isabella doing? My heart goes out to them. I'm heading to the sack now. It's been a long day. I'll be asleep before my head hits the pillow.

All the love a son can give,

Orrin

CHAPTER TWENTY-ONE

6 August 1953

Dearest Mother and Dad,

Go ahead and redecorate my bedroom. I appreciate the support you're giving Eloisa and Isabella. Once I return to the States, I will have to finish my commitment to the Navy and then on to medical school. I won't need a room for quite a while.

Well, Mother, I have some exciting news. I'm going to Japan for R&R tomorrow. Don't worry. Rawley will be with me. I'm going to call home if I can.

All the love a son can give,

Orrin

AFTER A BUMPY JEEP RIDE to Inchon, Orrin and I with a few other lucky men boarded a plane for Kyoto, Japan.

We each had two hundred dollars to spend. From the airport, we rode a military "cattle" truck to Camp Fisher on the outskirts of Kyoto.

We stared in awe at the green city spared from the bombs of WWII. Unlike Korea that had been blown to hell for years, Kyoto, built into the side of a small mountain, had green firs in its lush landscape. Our stress levels dropped a few notches. We quickly learned that Camp Fisher was a large Marine brig for Navy or Marine hooligans who had screwed up their R&R.

"I heard the Japanese call Camp Fisher the 'Big Monkey House,'" I said, eager to start our fun.

Standing in line with our R&R papers, Orrin and I discussed our plans. Well, I talked. Orrin listened.

"Basically, booze, girls, sleep," I said.

The other Marines nodded.

"What about food? A steak sounds good to me," Orrin said.

The Marines nodded again like giddy idiots.

"Right. Food, booze, girls, and sleep. In that order," I replied.

"Or any order," a nearby Marine added.

We took showers, hot showers. The water eased our aches and pains and washed away the grime of Korea and its emotional toll. In another line, we were fitted with khaki uniforms and then herded to the mess hall for hot chow and cold milk. Real milk, not powdered.

"Pass the milk," I said to the Marine next to the pitcher.

"I'll take more," Orrin said, putting his glass next to mine.

"Why does it taste like a milkshake?" a private asked, sliding his glass beside ours.

"It's the fat. Our bodies haven't had any for a while," I said, pouring milk into each. "We're craving it." Orrin carefully picked up his glass.

After dinner, the group headed to the barracks for early lights out. Nobody complained. We were lulled by the hot meal and cold milk. Most would have a busy five days. Orrin wanted to drink, relax, and shop for a gift for his mother's birthday. I wanted to have fun *dating*.

Happily up early, the group gathered in the mess hall for breakfast. Afterward, we remained seated and listened to Sergeant Spike yell a speech he'd probably repeated often.

"Listen up, you yahoos. For every American dollar, you get three hundred and sixty yen. Know the rate. Because prostitution is a legitimate business, there are twenty thousand prostitutes in Kyoto. Check their ID cards and don't get V.D. Keep your money and wits about you. If you cause a ruckus, you will do hard labor. I shit you not. Does everybody understand?"

"Yes Sergeant," we said in unison.

"Dismissed," he said.

The group scrambled for the exit. Taxis lined up outside the base. Orrin, tagalong Howard Gates, and I got into the eighth one, a clean cab driven by an old Japanese man.

"Kyoto Hotel?" he asked.

"Yes," I replied.

We passed temples and Shinto shrines. Bald Buddhist monks in red robes walked along the roads. The landscape was green and clean as though in Technicolor, not the drab dirty brown we were used to in Korea. The Kyoto Hotel for the enlisted men only was a thirteen-story R&R hotel, our home away from home. On the door, a sign read: GIRLS MUST BE ACCOMPANIED BY AMERICAN GI.

In the lobby with American decor, M.P.s watched for prostitutes and GI hijinks. The hotel staff, dressed in nice Western clothes, greeted us. The hotel had souvenir shops set up where we could purchase trinkets. The staff would even mail packages home for us. We wouldn't have to leave the hotel if we didn't want to, but we would.

Orrin and I paid extra for our own rooms. Howard Gates paid fifty cents a night for a cot on a lower floor. I planned on a different girl every night. Orrin didn't want to hear us. We had learned the top and tenth floors each had twelve-piece Japanese bands that played Glenn Miller music. We wouldn't mind forgetting the war for a few days.

After settling in his tiny private room, Orrin asked about calling home but there was a two-week waiting list. Before he could sulk, I pushed him toward the lobby door.

"I have five days to find just the right gifts for my sister and grandma," I said as we left the building.

For August, the breeze cooled our backs while we walked along the sidewalk. The smells of various food carts floated around us. Orrin's mood seemed to lighten at the beautiful city.

"What are you getting your parents?" I asked.

"I thought Mother would like a set of china. I'm not sure what to get my dad."

"We have five glorious days to find something. We'll know it when we see it," I said.

On the way back to the hotel, we were propositioned every four feet. I ate it up and flirted back. "They all want me."

Orrin rolled his eyes. "Because you have money."

I ignored the comment. "Here's your chance to practice."

"No, thanks. My mother would be in my head and that would scar me for the rest of my life."

I laughed. "Yikes. Is that why you didn't tell them ahead of time?"

"She means well, but I didn't want another lecture before we left. She's a nurse, you know."

I spotted a girl who interested me. "I'll meet you later for dinner and we'll get drunk," I said before greeting the pretty Japanese gal with her hair in a tight bun. Hand in hand, she and I entered the hotel.

The three of us looked at the souvenirs in the hotel lobby. Orrin picked up a tea cup from a ninety-three-piece set of blue and white china with a gold-plated design. He bought the set and then paid the extra to have it packaged and shipped home. While I took my date to my room, Orrin left to take a nap.

Later that night, on the dimly lit tenth floor, my date and I followed the hostess to a small round table for four away from the twelve-piece band playing Glenn Miller's "In the Mood". I ordered three Tom Collins and waited for Orrin to arrive. I waved him over as our waitress brought our drinks.

The tables quickly filled with enlisted men and their dates. Enjoying his drink and watching the dancing, Orrin tapped his toe to the music. I couldn't get over how soft my date's skin was. I had promised her one drink before I escorted her out. Yes, I'm a rogue.

"Vicar!" someone shouted over the music. "It's me, Nick Bradley." St. Nick, the religious Marine, walked toward our table.

"If I recall, you had a shoulder wound," Orrin said with a smile. I half-listened to their conversation.

"Yup, and you fixed me up—too good. I was sent back to my squad. But here I am still alive. Praise God." He sat down uninvited and flipped the switch on the table's center light, indicating we wanted service. "I owe you both a drink."

"Sure. Thanks," Orrin said. "How's your family?"

St. Nick winced and glanced in the direction of the girl he brought with him. I knew he wasn't the saint he'd led us to believe.

"Julie and the kids are well. Just letting off a little steam, is all," St. Nick replied.

Orrin nodded. "I remember your son was giving your wife some trouble."

"Oh right," he replied, surprised he remembered. "He's better now. I write to him separately. He just turned twelve, so I think he can handle the truths here."

Orrin nodded again. I frowned. I couldn't handle the truths here, but I didn't know St. Nick's son either. To each his own. I didn't pay much attention to St. Nick, who went on venting about his superiors, the so-called truce talks, and his violent patrols.

"I killed six gooks during one patrol," he boasted, puffing out his chest. "God's mighty hand on my gun."

Orrin downed his drink as St. Nick kept talking. By the time I returned from escorting my date to the lobby's front door, Orrin was drunk. His haunted look surprised me.

"What the hell is going on?" I demanded.

"Just talking about patrolling and killing," St. Nick said.

"Hell no! We're here to forget that shit." I leaned in inches from his face. "Go. Away."

We watched him sulk back to his date as I flipped the service switch. After one Tom Collins and two Sloe Gin Fizzes, Orrin still sat at attention. Was he stressed out? Of course, he was.

"We want two thick steaks with all the fixings," I said. She nodded and left. "Why didn't you tell him to shut the hell up?"

"He needed to vent," Orrin mumbled.

I shook my head. "You are too damn nice."

He smiled. "I guess it's a good thing you're here to corrupt me."

"I'm trying, man. I'm really trying," I replied with a laugh.

For the next four days, we stayed up until 0300, slept until 1100, walked around the city buying up trinkets, and then separated until dinner. I chose different girls each night, ditching them right after. At dinner, we ate, drank, and listened to the music. I made sure nobody talked about the war near us.

Before we knew it, we were on a plane back to Seoul. Three hours later, we loaded onto a train heading toward Able Med and the frontlines.

"Jesus, we're going two miles an hour," a nearby Marine said.

"You in a hurry to get to the front?" I asked. Orrin had his eyes closed and rocked with our slow-moving train.

"No, but—" he stammered.

"But nothing," another said. "I'm hoping with the armistice signed, we'll have nothing to do but twiddle our thumbs."

"Now wouldn't that be swell," I replied.

"So, the war's over? Why aren't we on the way home?" Howard Gates asked.

"How many times did we get excited about the truce talks ending the war?" I asked. "I'll tell you—a lot. Just because the armistice is signed doesn't mean the war is over. It just means they agreed to stop fighting until the final peace treaty is completed."

I made sure to keep up with the news. We argued back and forth, discussing what the armistice meant until the train jerked to a stop.

"What the hell?" I said, looking out the window. Rice paddies on the left, rocky hills on the right.

The Marines around us tensed. Some crouched down. Others looked for a weapon. Would this be our reaction to the suddenness of the world from now on?

A conductor came into our troop car. "Everybody out. We're switching trains."

"What do you mean?" a Marine asked.

"Some of the Army soldiers are going home."

Marines started swearing. With a sigh, Orrin gathered up his gear and switched to the train in front of us that would head back the way it had come to Able Med. We passed soldiers weary but smiling. The process slowed as they moved their wounded onto litters. Orrin glanced at me.

"Fine. We'll help them out," I said. "But if one of them rubs it in that they're going home, I'm going to lose it."

Orrin handed his gear to Gates. I shoved my gear at him, too.

"Don't go through my stuff. I'll know if you did," I said with a glare.

Orrin and I carried litters with soldiers to the train. There were sixty total heading home. None boasted. Instead, the men gave a nod wishing us a safe passage home, too. Once the train started moving toward the front again, the Marines continued to grumble.

Orrin finally spoke. "It'll be our turn soon and this nightmare will be over."

The group nodded and talked about the first thing we'd do when we got home. Orrin listened. Was Orrin just telling us what we needed to hear?

Would our nightmares dissipate once we returned home?

15 August 1953

Dearest Mother and Dad,

The first thing I did in Japan was see about calling home. They were booked for two weeks ahead of time. I'm so sorry, Mother. I did buy you a set of china and it should reach you in a few weeks. I hope you will like it. Boy, Kyoto was a beautiful place. They had more shrines and temples than you could shake a stick at.

Well, Mother, today was the longest day we have had since I have been in Korea. We have to stay here thirteen months. That means I won't be leaving until January, maybe longer. The drafts will be frozen over here even though the armistice was signed. Please don't stop writing.

All the love a son can give,

Orrin

CHAPTER TWENTY-TWO

30 August 1953

Dearest Mother and Dad,

I imagine it's hot in Amarillo. Same here. I could go for some of Grandma Pearl's homemade ice cream. Rawley and I argued about the best flavor. You know mine is vanilla. He loves chocolate. We both love cherry pie though. I can taste its sweet tartness just thinking about it.

Well, Mother, the china I bought you cost eighteen thousand yen; that comes to fifty dollars. Don't send me money. It's a gift for your birthday since I won't be home for it. Did Dad take you to dinner at Felton's Restaurant? I bet you had the rack of lamb and Dad had the porterhouse. I had a nice medium rare steak in Japan. It melted in my mouth.

Anyway, one of the guys here is going to Japan next week, so I'll have him pick up the pieces of china that arrived broken.

All the love a son can give,

Orrin

Orrin

SINCE THE SIGNING OF THE armistice on July 27th, we had been glued to the radio, praying we could go home. The officers had doubled down on discipline, protocol, and procedure. All the corpsmen, six now, continued to carry our carbines and medical bags all the time.

Constantly drenched in sweat, Rawley and I downed our chow in the mess tent so as not to be around the newer corpsmen. Somehow, we had become the seasoned ones. Drinking our coffee outside the tent, we looked around the plain, brown rocky terrain. The humidity and heat had taken the life out of everything, even the wilting rice paddies to the west. The field of barren dirt could only grow landmines to the east.

Rawley sighed. "Orrin, when we get home, I want you to visit me. I'll show you the boardwalk along the Kalamazoo River by the downtown buildings. It's surrounded by maple and oak trees. In May, the colorful flowers soothe your soul. I can't believe how much I miss it."

"Sounds like heaven," I replied.

"It really is."

In our quiet moment, a jeep from the south raced toward the camp. Dust kicked up behind it. Honking its horn, the driver broke through the security roadblock. Wood splinters flew high in the air. Two sentries ran after them. One shot out a tire, causing the driver to lose control. He smashed into the warning sign. Twenty yards into the field, a landmine flipped the jeep, catching it on fire.

"Go get the grid map for the field," Rawley said. He ran for the chaos.

I alerted the C.O., who quickly searched the file cabinet. Hearing another explosion, I felt a pit in my stomach and ran back to look. Rawley hadn't waited. Halfway to the jeep, he had stepped on a mine and lay next to the mini-crater.

"No. No. No," I said.

I ran past the onlookers who waited at the edge and carefully followed the tire tracks to my best friend. I knelt beside him. Shrapnel slashed his legs cutting deeply into his thighs. Dark blood flowed freely. I quickly applied tourniquets. My hands shook.

Dazed, Rawley stared at me.

"You want another medal that bad?" I asked. This was bad. Really bad.

"It doesn't hurt," Rawley whispered.

"Hey. Look at me. I'll get you out if I have to carry you out."

Calm washed over him as he paled. "I'm not going to make it. You need to help those others."

"I won't leave you." I pressed against the wounds, but blood soaked the ground.

"Tell my sister how brave I was." He smiled, then closed his eyes. "You're the best friend I ever..."

Just like that, he was gone. I vaguely heard the C.O. yelling to stay put. Covered in blood, I wept.

"Buck up, Connor," Doerr yelled. "Four paces forward."

I took a deep breath and glowered at the overturned jeep. Both men crushed under the weight. I stayed with Rawley. "They're dead," I said.

Rawley died for nothing. NOTHING!

Two Marines from ammunitions marked the mines to reach the jeep. Carrying a litter, corpsmen stopped beside me. I held Rawley's hand as Kunesh and Waters carefully placed him on it. I had no words. Did Rawley send me for the map, so I wouldn't run into the field? I was lost. I was destroyed.

Even with an armistice, men died. Senselessly. In a fog, I gathered Rawley's personal things. I thought about mailing the partially written letter to his sister, but for some reason it seemed cruel. I should write her. What would I say? *Your brother, my best friend, died trying to help two drunken Marines who drove into the middle of a minefield?* Tragic and painful. A part of me died, too. I wished it was me who died.

I stared at the silk scarf Rawley had bought his twin sister while on R&R. The scarf was soft against my rough hands. I carefully packed it in my bag, my excuse to visit the place Rawley called home—our last conversation.

Emotionally crippled, I hardened my resolve, carried my weapon, tended to the wounded in the ward, ate, slept, and repeated, all the while wondering how to write to Rawley's sister. I rewrote the letter four times.

8 September 1953

    Dear Ms. Armstrong,

    I'm Orrin Connor. Your brother was my best friend. I loved him, and I'm very sorry for your loss. He wasn't alone when he died. I was with him. He bravely tried to help our fellow Marines. As you know, it was in his nature to assist others. His good heart shone past his exterior gruff.

    With the herbs you had sent, he made the best chili I've ever had. All the guys love it as well as your homemade cookies and the other sweets.

    Rawley talked about home and his family often. I have gifts he bought special for you and your grandmother while we were in Japan. With your permission, I'd like to deliver them in person.

    I will miss your brother every day for the rest of my life.

    Orrin

CHAPTER TWENTY-THREE

14 September 1953

Dearest Mother and Dad,

No, Mother, I am not sure yet where I want to go to medical school. I have time. I don't mind sleeping on the couch. It'll be more comfortable than the cot I'm used to.

I'm happy you think Eloisa and Isabella are part of our family. I can't wait to try her empanadas. Sarino had said she was a great cook. I think it's wonderful you are teaching Isabella to paint. I love your artwork masterpieces. Dad, I'm glad you joined a bowling team. We'll bowl together when I get home.

It is getting chilly during the night. They are issuing our cold weather sleeping bags tomorrow. I'll write more soon.

All the love a son can give,
Orrin

UNDER THREE BLANKETS, I SHIVERED. I just couldn't get warm, even wearing my dungarees, boots, and coat. Would I ever be warm again? With my head under the blanket, I heard Kunesh kick the oil stove to jar it to work.

Bob Waters jumped up from his bunk. "Knock it off. You want to blow us up?"

I remembered that incident. Sciulli was gone, too. I understood why the veteran corpsmen were standoffish with the new men. I didn't want to meet anyone else either and start caring before they were killed. The emotional toll was painful.

I remained polite to Edward Allen, the Georgia boy that had been at the Battalion Reserve hospital with Kunesh, but I kept my distance. With more activity in our tent, I sighed and sat up. Colonel Doerr, our C.O., had us troop and stomp at 0530 every morning.

"The war's over and we're up an hour earlier than usual. This is stupid," Fitzpatrick said.

We agreed but still grabbed our gear for the morning's inspection. Six corpsmen stood at attention in the middle of the compound. The layers of my 782 gear—flak jacket, packs, canteen, poncho, ammo pouches, bandoliers, and carbines—barely kept me warm. We faced the minefield. I still couldn't look at it so I kept my eyes lowered.

This morning, General Berry from Battalion Reserve would inspect the corpsmen. Doerr stood at attention too and probably hoped we wouldn't make him look bad. Our laidback routine during the war had reverted back to the rigid structure of basic training. During the fighting, we knew our assignments and worked as one when the wounded arrived. Now, inspections seemed to give the officers something to do.

With my eyes averted from the minefield, I waited for the general to move down the line. Unaccustomed to inspections, Kunesh and Edward Allen stood so rigid I thought they would tip over. I wanted to whisper for them to unlock their knees, but I really didn't care. I just wanted to go home, although I wasn't sure I'd feel any better there.

"Why are your boots dusty?" Berry demanded.

Kunesh looked down. "Uh, the ground is dirty, sir." I cringed at his answer.

"No excuses." Berry turned to his lieutenant who held a clipboard. "On report."

Berry moved to Fitzpatrick and tugged on his medical pack untwisting it. "On report."

He stood in front of me. I had a lot of crooked layers. "When was the last time you used your weapon?" Berry asked.

"July 25th, sir," I replied.

"In battle?"

"Yes sir," I said.

"Well done," Berry replied.

I opened my mouth to reply that this whole war stunk but closed it. What good would it do? Rawley had mouthed off constantly and was always reprimanded for it.

"And you," Berry asked to Edward Allen. "Have you been in battle?"

"No sir, just Forward Aid," Allen replied.

"Maybe next time," Berry replied.

I considered that a battle zone. Forward Aid stations were set up on the rear slope where the fighting took place. Had General Berry ever seen action? Berry found something wrong with all of us. We were put on report for minor infractions.

Finally, he took the clipboard and scanned the sheet. "When I call your name, step forward," Berry said.

I braced for the military's version of asking for volunteers.

"Kunesh, Waters, Fitzpatrick, Connor." He thrust the clipboard back at his lieutenant. "You four are heading to the hospital ship for three days. The truck leaves at 1200. Dismissed."

The corpsmen put our gear in our tent and packed.

Maybe time away from Able Med would improve my morale and attitude.

The hard benches in the back of the truck numbed my butt during the long drive. The bouncing from the horrible dirt roads knocked Kunesh to the floor more than a few times. We left the back flap up until the dust choked us. Then, we put it down until the stagnant man smell gagged us. We couldn't find a happy medium.

Senior Corpsman Calvin Hackman greeted us at the Inchon dock. At 1400, we boarded a boat that shuttled us to the U.S.S. *Repose*. Hackman, a slim, rigid man in his thirties, lead us to our bunks to store our gear. Our dusty group didn't dare touch anything. The whole ship was immaculate, white, and shiny.

A hot shower, albeit a quick one, washed away my anger. Then chow in the mess hall of turkey, stuffing, and gravy with vanilla ice cream for dessert made me not want to weep. The crew ate like this all the time? No wonder Dr. Arrogant was jealous of the doctors here.

Relaxed and clean with full bellies, the Able Med corpsmen turned in early. We would observe the surgeries and protocol of the hospital ship early tomorrow morning.

Lying atop my bottom bunk, I anticipated the clean sheets, wearing only my skivvies. Much different at Able

Med where we all slept fully clothed, even with boots, in our sleeping bags.

While the P.A. System played the USC and Stanford football game, I closed my eyes and pretended I was at the Rose Bowl. Kunesh wrote home. Fitzpatrick and Waters played cards. I half-expected Rawley to look down at me from the upper bunk. In the doorway, a couple of the ship's corpsmen looked around our area.

"Uh, hey, we're looking for the Vicar," the lanky one said, smoothing down his pants that were as long as I was tall.

"Did he make the trip?" the chubby one asked. His uniform tight around the middle.

Fitzpatrick, Waters, and Kunesh pointed at me. I leaned on my elbow and waved them in. "What can I do for you?"

The men looked at each other then sat on the empty bunk across from me. I shook their hands as they introduced themselves. Curious, the others leaned toward me to hear the conversation.

"We thought you'd be older," chubby Carl Anderson said.

"Older?" I asked. Able's corpsmen laughed.

"And bigger," tall Ben Colby added.

"Why?" I asked.

"We've heard stories about the Vicar. You've become a legend around here," Anderson said. Able's corpsmen nodded and smiled.

"Again why?" I asked, embarrassed by the attention.

"You saved a lot of men who came through here," Anderson said.

"Sergeant Mayo said you saved his life," Colby said.

"How is he?" I asked.

"Glad to be alive," Anderson said.

"That's wonderful," I replied, looking at the corpsmen moving closer. "We never hear how the men are doing after they leave Able Med. Can you tell me how Johnny Johnson and Major Webster are doing?"

"Johnson is paralyzed from the waist down but has movement is his arms. He's with his daughter and wife back in the States," Colby said. "And Webster will make a full recovery, thanks to you, and so will Hey Baby Marshall."

"My buddy, Rawley Armstrong, aided them, too," I said, remembering Webster's collapsed lung and Marshall's numb arm in the field. I asked about a few more.

By lights out, I was relieved to hear so many men were alive and doing well. Our service wouldn't be forgotten, at least, not by those men.

22 September 1953

Dearest Mother and Dad,

I spent a few days touring the U.S.S. Repose, the hospital ship just off Inchon. Boy, they have the best equipment, but I would just as soon serve a shorter time in Korea than twenty-four months on the hospital ship.

I'm back at the new Able Med. We've moved farther back from the MRL. I just finished chow—not as good as on the ship—so I had a few minutes to write.

They keep us busy here with inspections. The officers don't want us to let our guard down in case something negates the armistice agreement.

Hello. I'm back again. I had to pause a moment to hear the announcements. I'm afraid I have to disappoint you again. The dispatch said there won't be another corpsmen draft going home until the end of December. It looks as if I will spend more than a year in Korea. Please, keep writing to me.

All the love a son can give,

Orrin

CHAPTER TWENTY-FOUR

26 October 1953

Dearest Mother and Dad,

The list came out today of those who made Second Class. Yup, I made it, which means more money for my savings and I finally know what kind of car I want.

Dad, I'm sorry to hear Uncle Ned passed away. I know what it's like to lose someone you're close to. Please send my love to Aunt Myrna, Jimmy, and George.

I want to mail this out so I'm saying goodbye for now. I sure hope I get a letter today. I'll write more soon.

All the love a son can give,

Orrin

I SEALED THE ENVELOPE THEN slipped on my poncho. From the tent doorway, I watched as the cold rain pounded the ground. A river of water rushed down the hill into the mess tent at the bottom.

The new Able Med was reestablished on the side of a large hill with narrow inclines. The corpsmen's and doctors' tents were on the top. Just below us, about fifty feet straight down, were two wards. Below those were the admissions, x-ray, and minor and major surgeries in a large F-shaped building. With the last two days of hard rain, the mud ran into all the buildings, ruining the place. Doerr was still a dummy for moving us here.

I watched Kunesh struggle to climb the hill. For every two steps, he slid down three. At least going down would be easier. With a sigh, I half-slid, half-walked toward the mess tent at the very bottom. As I smiled that I made it without wiping out, I missed a step and landed in the mud, which seeped into my poncho pockets. My mood soured at my muddy wet envelope. I'd have to wait and rewrite it.

Inside the mess, I flapped my poncho to rid the excess water. The mud had infiltrated everything. We gave up keeping ourselves clean. At least today, we wouldn't have inspections. Doerr didn't like standing in the rain either.

Caleb Fitzpatrick stood on a bench with a large stack of letters and a few packages. Surrounding him, Marines anticipated a letter from home. I waited to hear my name. I had hoped for a response to a letter I mailed last month.

The crowd thinned. I remained. Maybe I missed the first call.

"Did I get anything?" I asked.

"No, sorry," Fitz replied, hopping down. "Maybe tonight. I heard a PX truck's coming in."

I nodded, then grabbed a mug of coffee and two oatmeal cookies, wrapping them in individual napkins. I had no appetite. I worried over the anticipated letter.

Holding my mug under my poncho, I slid the cookies into my pocket then walked with care back up to the ward. Mine had two Marines with shrapnel injuries from an accidental ammunitions explosion. Two other men had died needlessly. I knew what that felt like. The thought fouled my mood more.

I set my coffee on the table and shook out my poncho again. Replacing Eddie Allen for the day's watch, I met him in the corner away from the two men.

"I just gave them their pain meds and rebandaged their wounds. Healing well," Allen said, shifting his stance. "But—"

I nodded for him to continue.

"Keep an eye on Miller. Something's not right with him."

"Depression?" I asked. Allen nodded.

Private Ken Miller wasn't the first to feel that way. I had heard doctors call it "survivor's guilt." Having a name for it didn't make it any better. I sipped my lukewarm coffee then set the mug aside. Sitting on a stool beside Miller, I pulled out the two cookies. I handed one to him and set the other on Corporal Seth Jones' bedside table for when he woke up.

"I heard you'll be heading home soon," I said.

Miller bit into the cookie. "Not soon enough."

"I know," I said, leaning forward. My elbows resting on my lap, I stared at my hands. "I lost my best friend after the armistice was signed. So senseless," I whispered. Would sharing with a fellow Marine help him cope? I had no idea.

"Two of our brothers in my squad died," Miller choked out, dropping the cookie onto his blanket. "How the hell do we make sense of any of this?"

"I guess we find a reason to live again," I said.

From the other bed, Seth Jones turned on his side to face us. "I hate the enemy so much."

"My dad said when he was in WWII, it was the politics of war he despised. The enemy we see does what they're told, just like we do," I said.

"I suppose so," Jones said.

"What's the first thing you're going to do when you get home?" I asked, changing the disheartening conversation.

"Make love to my wife," Jones said.

Miller and I smiled. "That beats a banana split," I said.

"Yes. Yes, it does. I can't wait to hug her," Jones replied.

"Stop rubbing it in," Miller said, chuckling. He munched on his cookie again. "Connor, what are your plans after the war?"

"Well, I have to finish my commitment to the Navy, then medical school, I guess. What about you?"

"My dad owns a grocery store in Newton, New Jersey. I'll help him. May even take over for him someday," Miller replied.

"I'm not sure what I'll do. Not staying in the Marines, that's for sure," Jones said.

"If you were, I'd have Connor take an x-ray of your skull," Miller said, laughing.

The P.A. System cracked on. I tensed as a reflex. "Attention, Able Med. The twenty-seventh draft of corpsmen will be shipped home November nineteenth."

I teared up. "I'm going home," I whispered.

"Congratulations," Miller said.

"You may leave before us, Vicar," Jones replied.

I couldn't wait to write home. Letting the men rest and daydream, I finished my paperwork. At lunch, I carried three trays back to the ward for my two patients and me. I passed Kunesh who couldn't stop smiling. I was excited too, but kept it in check. Many weren't leaving yet.

I chatted on and off with the men until I heard the PX truck stop at the base of our hill. Hoping the mail arrived too, I asked the men if they wanted anything.

"Chocolate," Jones said. Miller nodded.

I slipped my poncho back on and practically ran to the truck. Fitzpatrick beat me there and had a bundle of mail to pass out. I quickly bought a couple of candy bars and followed Fitz into the mess tent. Just as the rats followed the music of the pied piper, the Marines chased the letters.

Fitzpatrick called out four names, then mine. He sniffed it. "Smells good, Connor."

They all looked at me and smiled. I turned bright red and grabbed my letter. After delivering the chocolate, I turned my back to them and sniffed the letter. It really did smell good. I wanted the inside to be just as good. Alone at the table in the ward, I took a deep breath, then slowly blew it out. Why was I so nervous?

16 October 1953

Dear Orrin,

Thank you for your letter. I'm glad he wasn't alone. My grandmother and I would like to meet you in person. In the spring. If you have leave. Michigan winters are too harsh for a Texas boy like you. Spring here is my favorite season. Everything is in bloom.

From Rawley's letters, we feel you are already a part of our family. Write me again to let us know when you're coming. You can stay at the boarding house. We look forward to your visit.

Sincerely,

Gail Armstrong

CHAPTER TWENTY-FIVE

3 November 1953

> *Dearest Mother and Dad,*
>
> *In fourteen more days, I will be leaving Korea for good. We will arrive in San Francisco on the third of December. I'll have to spend a week or more processing for leave, but I'm hoping to be home with you for Christmas. By the time you receive this, I'll be on my way to the States so you should stop writing because I won't get them.*
>
> *All the love a son can give,*
> *Orrin*

PER GENERAL BERRY'S ORDERS, ALL the Marines in the area were to have physicals, which meant x-rays. I looked out the radiology tent. Fifty Marines, antsy and impatient, stood in line. Oh, boy! Well, at least it was a sunny day. In charge, I had Kunesh and Waters helping supposedly to keep the process running smoothly.

Arrogant and angry, Major Daniels entered through the side door. "I need a corpsman to assist in an appendicitis surgery."

I immediately felt my stomach knot up. I had avoided surgeries since visiting the U.S.S. *Repose*. Observing the blood and guts had me green. I had struggled not to throw up, especially when those corpsmen referred to me as a *legend*—a stupid legend. Ridiculous. Then the nightmares filled my head. How was I supposed to become a doctor? I still pictured every Marine who'd died, and I still saw Rawley bleeding in the minefield whenever I closed my eyes.

Waters volunteered. Thank goodness. With a grateful sigh, I used my clipboard to fill out the paperwork while Kunesh did the actual x-rays. Hearing a commotion outside, I opened the door. The long line of Marines was pushing and shoving, arguing and fighting. The process was taking too long for these blockheads.

For the first time as a corpsman, I channeled my inner Sergeant Mayo and shouted, "Listen up, shitheads. Knock it the hell off."

The men, all of whom were twice as big as I was, stopped and stared, clearly surprised by my outburst.

On a roll, I kept shouting. "We're going as quickly as we can, so stand there and think about your answer to this question: What's the first thing you're going to do when you get home? When it's your turn, I want a thoughtful answer."

Someone in the back said, "And what if we don't have a thoughtful answer?"

"May I remind you that I have access to your medical records. Would you rather have gonorrhea, the clap, or crabs?" The crowd silenced and I did an about-face.

The next Marine inside the tent stared. "You'd really do that?"

"Of course not. It's against the law to falsify records," I replied. The Marine laughed. "Well, what's your answer, Corporal?"

"Oh, after my six months are up, I'm going to school. I'm good with numbers and thought I could be a bookkeeper."

"A thoughtful answer," I said, handing him the paperwork I had filled out for him.

I heard the men sharing their answers outside where they joked and laughed. I continued to spend the day filling out paperwork and listening to answers, which ranged from various jobs and getting married to a fresh egg omelet and a thick, juicy steak. The ones who chose the food items quickly backed up their answers with their life's plan.

Colonel Doerr joined me at the end of our shift. "I saw what you did, Connor. Well done."

"Thank you, sir. Sometimes thinking about a positive future dulls the temporary frustration of the present."

"You'll make a fine doctor," Doerr replied before a corporal distracted him with his own paperwork.

The thought made my gut ache. I liked talking to the men, getting to know them, but the rest filled me with dread. I should take my own advice. My thoughtful plan seemed to be falling apart. I needed to buck up or it would hurt a lot of people—well, mostly my parents.

The day finally came. Kunesh and I shook hands with those left behind. Some were happy for us; others angry that they weren't leaving, too. I understood that.

Loaded in the back of a transport truck with Kunesh and a few Marines, we headed to Inchon. I stared at a similar spot in the rocky dirt of the minefield. I couldn't turn away. I was going home. My best friend was not.

The only solace was my planned visit to meet Rawley's sister and grandmother. They loved him, too, and would understand my pain. My heart was full of sorrow. I had done horrible things in the name of war. How would I live with myself?

Lugging our gear, we boarded the train an hour later. Our troop car, filled with men going home, was loud with jovial banter. As much as I wanted to go home, I was also terrified. I was different. Would my family be able to tell? Would they see my internal scars?

At Inchon, I gladly turned in my 782 gear. A Marine handed me a pressed uniform for my homecoming. Many family members would be there to welcome the men home. I'd see my parents at Christmas and that was good enough for me.

We waited in another long line to board the U.S.S. *Kearsarge*—a sight for sore eyes. This time, I wasn't at the bottom of the hole, but nearer the top. I chose to help in the kitchen, forgoing sickbay. My passion for medicine was gone.

Sitting on an upside-down bucket, I peeled potatoes with two others. I laughed at their jokes to be polite. I'd had more fun with Rawley. As I thought about the differences without my buddy, Corporal Cinder said something.

"Sorry," I said. "What did you say?"

"Do you have family meeting you? If not, you're welcome to join us. We're going to dinner and then dancing."

I lied. "Thank you, but my family will be there." I did not want to be around a bunch of drunken Marines.

The men chatted about home while my mind drifted. I also thought about Rawley and Sciulli's rivalry. That had eventually changed, too. I understood why the men would drink, numbing their pain. I decided never to drink again. A drunk driver had indirectly killed my best friend. I could no longer have alcohol without thinking about that scene. Although, I suspect that moment would always be in the forefront of my mind. Nonetheless, it was a way to honor Rawley. I had no idea how I would numb my pain, though.

As the day neared, I planned to grab a hot dog on the pier. My life decisions had plagued me with insomnia. After twelve days on the ship, I still had no idea what I wanted to do. Luckily, I didn't have to decide until my commitment was completed a whole year from now. I just didn't know what to tell my parents over my Christmas break.

The U.S.S. *Kearsarge* neared San Francisco Bay and the Golden Gate Bridge. In clean uniforms, we carried our sea bags and found a spot along the railing up top. The cool wind whipped across the deck. Nobody cared. We searched the crowd.

Young and old greeted us along the boardwalk. I felt the excitement. The lucky ones were returning to their families. The men formed a line to disembark and find their sweeties. I let them go first. I smiled at all the hugs given out.

Then I blinked. I spotted my parents. Colonel Charles Connor MD and Mrs. Helen Connor waited next to the gate below. Wearing a brown suit, my dad had a hand at my mother's back as she clutched her purse to her chest. I teared up. I wanted to return to my innocence—the wide-eyed kid with a passion to help others. Now, at nineteen, that felt like a lifetime ago.

I embraced my mother. She smelled like roses from her favorite perfume.

"We've missed you so," she said.

"I've missed you, too," I said, releasing her. I hugged my dad.

"Are you surprised?" Dad asked.

"Yes! I didn't think I'd see you until Christmas."

"Eloisa and Isabella are at the house," Mother said. "She didn't want to come."

"I understand," I replied.

"We have dinner reservations at the ritzy hotel in town," Dad said.

Arm in arm with my mother, I walked with them toward the parking lot. "I can ride with you over to Treasure Island to the U.S. Naval facility. I'll get paid and liberty for the night. Then I'll spend about five days for more processing before I get leave for Christmas." I gently pulled my mother closer. "What a wonderful surprise!"

My parents patiently waited with me in line. Fewer corpsmen from the twenty-seventh draft returned home. With his pocket full of money, Kunesh passed me and waved.

"See you tomorrow, Vicar," he said.

"Be safe," I replied, taking a step closer to the front of the line. Only five ahead of us.

"Vicar?" Mother asked.

"Apparently, I'm a good listener."

She smiled. "You get that from your father. It's a plus with patients, especially if they're veterans."

I nodded, keeping my lips pursed together. Deep breaths.

"Using the G.I. bill, you can choose any university you want," Dad added.

"I still have a year to go."

"It's never too early to get the ball rolling," Mother said.

"Yes, ma'am," I replied, stepping closer. Third in line. How can I change the subject?

"The hotel will have a band playing. I thought we could cut a rug to celebrate your homecoming," Dad interjected.

"Will you dance with me, Mother?" I asked, relieved to talk about something else.

"I'd love to," she replied, patting my cheek.

Finally seated in the posh ballroom, I looked around. Other families with their returning military loved ones filled the room.

"Should we order champagne?" Dad asked.

I winced. "If you don't mind, I'd really like a tall glass of cold milk."

My dad laughed. "Of course. I remember my first meal after being a POW. The milk was creamy and rich."

"Like a milkshake," I added.

The waiter arrived and Mother ordered three glasses of cold milk. Did my dad and I have more in common than I thought?

After our steak dinners, we danced and laughed and enjoyed our night as a family, forgetting the past and the future. Their silent support focusing on the present meant the world to me. I was sincerely grateful they had come. It touched my heart. I couldn't disappoint them now.

20 December 1953

Dear Gail,

Merry Christmas. I know it will be a tough one. I will be praying for you and your grandmother.

My next leave will begin May 1ˢᵗ. It will take me a few days to get there. I'm looking forward to the visit. I've included my new address. Please write if there is an issue with the date.

Sincerely,

Orrin Connor

CHAPTER TWENTY-SIX

1 May 1954

Dearest Mother and Dad,

I'm going on a road trip to Michigan for a week or so. I have some unfinished business there. I'm delivering Rawley's gifts to his sister and grandmother. I promise to stop in before heading back to the base.

All the love a son can give,

Orrin

I COULDN'T WAIT TO GET on the road in my new 1953 Chevy Bel Air. My four-door, green machine had a white roof and shiny chrome. A driving dream. I enjoyed springtime in the Midwest. I only had three speeding tickets to prove it. The police had stopped me six separate times on my road trip from California to Michigan. I gladly paid them.

The closer I got to Allenton, Michigan, the more nervous I became. I had gone over my speech since San Francisco. Now, it sounded stupid. I wasn't much for ad-libbing. The main reason I wrote letters was so I wouldn't get tongue-tied.

The beautiful area distracted me. Rawley had said the spring greenery would lift my spirits. I agreed. With my window down, I smelled lilacs as I slowly drove down the street. Colorful impatiens decorated the large blue boarding house with a wraparound porch near the center of the town. Large oak trees shaded the white picket fence surrounding the small front yard. The light blue sky framed the epitome of spring.

In my pressed khaki uniform, I carried my sea bag up the three steps to the front porch. Hearing voices inside, I peeked through the screen door. Wearing a floral dress, a young woman with short, curly chestnut hair had her hands on her curvy hips. She stood in front of the neighborhood boy, maybe ten years old.

"Steven Nickolson, did you eat that tart that was cooling on the kitchen table?" she said.

He shook his head as cherry filling dripped down his chin. I smiled.

"You're a bad liar. Get out before I paddle your behind," she said.

Steven ran past her and out the screen door.

"Was getting in trouble worth it?" I asked.

Grinning with cherry tart covering his teeth, he nodded and jumped off the top step of the porch. When I turned back, Gail stared at me. She smoothed down her dress and then the rogue curl by her ear.

"Hi. I'm Orrin."

"I know."

She hesitated for a second, then launched herself at me. She squeezed me and buried her face against my shirt. I held her as she cried. I struggled not to.

"I'm so sorry," I whispered. "I loved him."

"He loved you. He told me so in his letters." She stepped back and wiped her face. "You were very good to him."

I laughed—a genuine laugh. The first time in a long time. "I tried to be, but his mouth got him into trouble often."

She smiled. "That sounds about right. Stay right here. I want to find Grandma. She'll want to hug you, too."

I smiled and nodded like a dimwit. Gail raced into the kitchen while I looked around their parlor. I honed in on the mantel where they had placed Rawley's Navy picture, a tri-folded American flag, his dog tags, and his medal.

I looked closer at a few snapshots stuck to the wall. I remembered posing for the group photo of all the corpsmen at Able Med when we first arrived. I had the same picture. The other was me and Rawley just before a patrol. We wore all our heavy gear. Rawley had said it was as light as a feather. The box his medal came in had a brass plate inside that said *Corpsman 3rd Class, Rawley Matthew Armstrong.*

Wiping away a tear, I opened my bag and pulled out two wrapped rectangular boxes. I felt a great responsibility to deliver them and was happy to do it.

Seventy-year-old Minnie Armstrong entered the room. Short and round, she wiped her hands on her apron. She bear-hugged me. For a tiny woman, she had a grip.

"I'm so sorry you lost your friend," she said.

I teared up. Nobody had ever said that to me. I cleared my throat. "Thank you," I whispered.

She stood back and smiled. "Gail, fetch our guest some iced tea."

Gail disappeared, and Minnie took my hand and gently led me to the sofa in the parlor. The whole house had a warm, cozy feel with its eclectic furniture. My parents' house had one specific style: Old English.

"Rawley grew up here?" I asked, discreetly wiping my eye.

"Since he and Gail turned five," Minnie said. "It broke our hearts when we heard he died."

"Yes, ma'am. I was with him. He rushed in to save a couple of Marines."

Before the conversation got too heavy, I placed the two gifts on the coffee table. Gail returned and set down the tray of iced tea and cherry tarts.

"How long can you stay?" Gail asked.

"A couple of days, if that's all right with you both."

"Stay as long as you like," Minnie said.

"Which one is mine?" Gail asked, sitting on the edge of her chair. She nervously smoothed out the part of her dress on her lap.

I leaned over and picked up the pink box. I passed it to her. My hand touched her fingers. Startled, she fell off her chair landing hard on the floor. I jumped up to help her. Minnie cackled at her then grabbed the other box. She opened hers and found a deep purple silk scarf.

"Oh my, I love purple." Minnie glanced at the mantle. "Thank you, Rawley."

Pink-faced, Gail tore open hers, averting her eyes from me. It amused me. She gasped at the Kelly-green silk scarf.

"I love this color," she said, putting it around her neck.

"Lovely," I said. "Rawley said it's the color of spring, your favorite season."

Dismissing the tea and tarts, the gals touched the silk, admiring the colors. I enjoyed the scene and felt Rawley loved it, too. He had said as much when he bought them in Kyoto.

"Gail, why don't you show Orrin his room? He's probably tired from the trip. We can talk more at dinner."

Gail stood and I followed her up the stairs to the first room on the left.

"Um, I have a gift for you from Rawley," she said, wringing her hands.

"Really? I can't imagine what it would be. I was with him when we shopped."

"Would you like to see the town first?" she asked.

"Sure. He talked about the boardwalk."

She nodded. "I'll let you settle in. Come downstairs when you're ready.

"Thank you, Gail."

I quickly put my clothes in the empty dresser. I liked this room with its full-sized feather bed, rocking chair, bedside table, and homemade rug on the wood floor. A colorful assortment of tiny flower designs covered the wallpaper, and the bed had a homemade quilt of triangular pieces. It looked much more comfortable than a thin mattress on a Navy cot.

After glancing down the hallway to the shared bathroom for the upstairs boarders, I found Gail sitting in a wicker chair on the porch. Just inside the door, I watched her smooth down her dress again. She crossed her legs, then uncrossed them before sitting up straighter.

I sat in the chair beside her. She remained quiet. "What's on your mind?" I asked. Instead of answering, she handed me a box—the one Rawley's medal came in. I didn't take it. "I don't want Rawley's medal."

She opened it then showed me. I looked at the name on the brass plate: *Corpsman 3rd Class Orrin Stanley Connor.* I was shocked.

"Rawley dug it out of the trash and sent it to me with instructions to give it to you in person. He said, 'You may be reminded of the men who died, but what about all the men you saved? You gave those men a future.' My brother wrote how brave you were many times while on patrol. He wrote me all about what you went through, and if you want to talk about it, I'm here for you."

I struggled to get my emotions under control. "I killed men," I blurted out.

"Rawley knew you did that for him. He also had told me you're in pain because of it, but I know your goodness will radiate, whatever you decide to do with your life."

I took a deep breath and let it out. "Your brother and I had debated about sharing or withholding our experiences in the war through the letters we wrote home. He clearly wins. I can hear him calling me a knucklehead."

Gail laughed. "His favorite word. I told him it would be a spiritual healing to his soul."

I nodded. "I feel better already."

"Well, good. Let's go for a walk," she said. "You don't have to share if you don't want to."

"Thank you. Do you think when we get back, I can try a tart? I have a feeling they're delicious." I nodded toward the hedge where Steven waited to sneak back into the kitchen.

Gail took a step in his direction. "When we get back, there had better be five left."

Steven stood and smiled.

Gail looked at me. "I left six cooling on the counter."

I laughed. "You're a softy."

"Don't tell anyone. I have a mean reputation to uphold."

She reached for my hand as we walked down the sidewalk. I knew she was bossy. I didn't mind. I also knew her favorite flowers were impatiens. She loved Kelly green and the spring season. Rawley had talked about his sister and grandmother often. I paid attention. I liked her before I ever met her. I had a feeling Rawley knew I did.

"Do you think I could write to you?" I asked, feeling bold. I still held my breath.

"Only if you share the truth with me. You can start by writing about the day Rawley died, up until now. Can you do that?"

"Yes, I think I can." I squeezed her hand and pulled her a little closer.

7 *May 1954*

Dearest Mother and Dad,

I love you. Your letters of support while in Korea have meant the world to me. I am sorry to say I must disappoint you. I have changed my plans, long-term and short-term.

I'm staying in Michigan a little longer to help Rawley's grandmother with a few projects at her boarding house, and I've met someone who understands. I've had a hard time since Rawley died. His sister, Gail, is easy to talk to. She is the one for me. I know Rawley would approve.

After my commitment to the Navy is finished, I've decided not to go to medical school. Since the war, I'm not passionate about it anymore. I will figure out another way to help people.

I hope and pray that you will understand.

All the love a son can give,

Orrin

20 May 1954

Dearest Son,

We are not disappointed in you. I have read between the lines since you left for Korea. During WWII in the prison camp, I saw the horrors of war, too. I also did what I had to do to protect my men. I couldn't share it with anyone, thinking nobody would understand—not even your mother. I am glad you found someone who understands. I'd never tell you not to write to your mother, but you can write separately to me if you'd like.

Please, don't stop writing to us. We are so proud of you.

With love,

Dad

EPILOGUE

IN THE MIDDLE OF THE living room empty of furniture, Eva read aloud the last letter Orrin's dad had written. She wiped her eyes. They gaped at the items David had set out during Eva's narration. Stacks of handwritten envelopes, two small, gray boxes containing "Letter of Commendation" medals, two purple hearts, a tri-folded American flag given to Gail after Rawley died, and two dog tags.

The three sets of letters told the whole story. Rawley's to his sister gave them the horrible truths of the war. Orrin's to his parents showed a son's love shielding them from his pain. And Orrin's letters to Gail, sharing a bond about his life after Rawley.

"Dad, you never knew about this?" David asked.

Matt shook his head then stared at the front door for a moment. "Dad always winced when the P.A. System cracked on at the beginning of my high school football and basketball games. And he hated fireworks."

"Oh, wow," David said. "I just realized. When Grandpa took me fishing, it was Grandma who showed me how to gut and clean the fish. Do you think the war was the reason Grandpa wouldn't do it?"

"It could be. It makes more sense now," Matt replied. "I wish he would have shared his story."

"In a way, he did." David gestured to the letters and memorabilia scattered around them. "I am so getting an *A* on my family tree project for school."

Matt had thought he was close to his father. Maybe they hadn't been. Or had his dad shielded him like he did his parents?

In the end, though, Orrin had helped many people in their town as a mail carrier, observing and lending a hand wherever needed. He had found his purpose. Matt understood now.

Thank you, Dad. I miss you.

XXX

Thank you for your service

Lieutenant Colonel John Bunyan Bennett, M.D.,
United States Army (WWI, WWII)

Parachute Rigger 1st Class LeRoy Stewart Thompson,
United States Navy (WWII)

Hospital Corpsman 2nd Class Hershall Floyd Bennett,
United States Navy/Marines (Korean War)

Senior Airman James Hershall Bennett,
United States Air Force

Corporal Caleb Weyrick-Greene,
United States Marines (Afghanistan)

Senior Airman David Stuart Thompson,
United States Air Force

Other Titles by Christina Thompson

The Trucker's Cat

The Garden Collection

Their Rigid Rules
(The Chemical Attraction Series Book 1)

The Kindred Code
(The Chemical Attraction Series Book 2)

Searching for Her: an anthology of short stories
(The Chemical Attraction Series Book 2.5)

Chemical Attraction
(The Chemical Attraction Series Book 3)

Chemical Reaction
(The Chemical Attraction Series Book 4)

About the Author

As a former holistic practitioner with a science background, Christina Thompson enjoys writing about the physical science, the emotional workings of our mind and heart, and the spiritual energy that taps into our passions.

Her degree in biology from Nazareth College in Kalamazoo gave her a love of science and a background into the physical realm of the body. Her diploma in Traditional Chinese acupuncture from Midwest College of Oriental Medicine taught her that the mind and spirit affect the body in powerful ways. She currently resides with her husband, Kraig, in Michigan.

For more information on the Eclectic Life of Christina, visit **ChristinaKThompson.com**.

Made in the USA
Columbia, SC
01 June 2021